RETRIBUTION
and Other Stories

JJ TONER

Contents

INTRODUCTION

These stories range in setting from Earth to outer space to heaven, and from the nineteenth century to the far distant future. They have one thing in common: They are all about crime.

Some of the stories were written in British English, others in US English.

THE MEAT IN THE SANDWICH

First published in Noir Nation 3, 2013 and
Knife Edge, 2013

Realtors are a shifty lot, but the one that sold me this
place couldn't look me in the eye for more than a second. I
made a ludicrously low offer and he jumped at it. I should
have guessed right then that there was trouble ahead.

The place looked fine: a bright, spacious store well sit-
uated on the corner of Jefferson and L. It looked perfect.
And it had a good-sized storeroom out back.

About a week after I'd opened, a wide black dude comes
into the store in a white suit. Speaking like Paul Robeson,
he says there's a lot of crime about. Looters everywhere,
windows can get smashed, fires start so easily. He's selling
insurance, and it's gonna cost me three grand, payable the
first Monday of each month.

There's a psychiatric condition called Pathological Demand Avoidance. I reckon I must have it. I get palpitations
when anyone asks me for money. Anyway, there was no
way I could stump up that sort of green. I told him to take
a hike.

***

The next day, it's two whiteys offering the same service for five. Peas in a pod these two, wearing matching hats and Armani suits. One of them delivers the message at fifty dollars a word. The other one stands around like a mortician's mate measuring me for my coffin.

I said, "You're too late, guys. I signed up with a black firm only yesterday."

"Not our problem," says the talkative one. "Collection day's first Tuesday of the month. *Capiche?*"

I began to realize why the place had been so cheap. It straddled the territories of two rival gangs, and both gangs had a claim on it.

Who wants to be the meat in the sandwich?

I rang Bubba.

Bubba's not your average Joe, not unless your average Joe is six foot four, two hundred pounds of solid Samoan muscle with a heart the size of Ellis Island and a face that curdles goats milk. Bubba's a good friend. When I first met him he was an Olympic silver medalist at the start of a promising professional boxing career. I was manager of a multi-million-dollar investment fund. That was in the days when even boys with paper rounds had a portfolio of dodgy commodities and the whole world was living in cloud-cuckoo land. Bubba's sports management company had given him a handsome sign-on fee and Bubba came to me for advice. I advised him to invest in steel, but he went into rubber. When the stock market crashed my investment fund collapsed, but he bounced back.

I laid out my problem, and Bubba scratched his knuckles. When Bubba puts his brain in gear he always scratches his knuckles. I reckon his brains must be in his fingers.

After about five minutes' serious knuckle-scratching he reached a conclusion. "You'll have to call the cops."

I objected. The last thing I wanted was to get the mobs riled.

"It's a no-brainer, Pete," he said. He always called me 'Pete'. Not sure why. My name's Barney.

I slipped him a couple of six-packs and a carton of Moroccan smokes and rang the cops.

***

The two patrolmen could have come from the same pond as the Italians. Probably played golf in the same club. The only real difference was that these two wore their guns on their belts. And they had a habit of finishing each other's sentences.

They introduced themselves as patrolmen Burke and Kerrigan of the twenty-second precinct. I gave them the highlights of my week so far.

"Sounds like Pinky Sparrow," said Burke.

"And Montalbano's mob," said Kerrigan.

I said, "I told the Italians that I'd already signed up with the other lot. They weren't interested. They said they'd be round to collect the first Tuesday of every month."

Kerrigan scratched his nose. "Could you manage three?"

"No way. I'm already fully stretched at the bank."

Burke handed me a dog-eared card.

Kerrigan said, "Just call that number if you need us."

***

The last day of September was a Saturday. Thoughts of the week ahead were sending creeper crawlers abseiling up and down my spine.

I rang the number the cops had given me, and what sounded like a sixth-grader told me that Burke and Kerrigan were on rotation.

"What does that mean?" I said.

"It means they're on nights. I can pass on a message if you like."

"Forget it, sonny," I said and slammed the phone down.

I rang Bubba and left a message on his phone.

***

By Sunday morning I'd heard nothing from Bubba. I drove round to his house on lower east side and knocked on the door. No one answered.

A dumpy woman appeared on the stoop next door, dressed in a plastic apron, her hair tied up in a scarf. It was a pretty scarf. "Bubba's away on a hunting trip," she said.

I flashed an image of Bubba in the woods, knocking down trees with his shoulders, trying to sneak up on some unsuspecting game.

A knot was forming in my stomach. I was on my own, facing the imminent prospect of confrontations with not one, but two criminal gangs. My livelihood was under threat, and if I stood my ground, limbs were likely to get broken.

My limbs.

What I needed was a plan.

I ran through various scenarios in my head. There was Barney the Kung-Fu specialist. How quickly can you learn a martial art? Barney the Invisible Man and Barney the Superhero were just wishful thinking, Barney the gunman …

I liked that idea. I could buy myself a gun, maybe a pump-action, and keep it behind the counter. But then I saw the worm in that apple. It takes several weeks—two at least—to buy a gun. There are forms to fill in, checks to be made.

I settled on the only plan that had any chance of success: Barney the lily-livered craven coward.

I shut up shop.

Down the street, on the opposite side from my store, there's a coffee bar. First thing Monday morning, I bought a latte and bagel and took them to a table in the window where I could watch the door of my store.

Five lattes and three bagels later, Pinky Sparrow arrived. He tried the door before ambling off down the road, swinging his hips like a $20 trick.

Too nervous to open the store, I decided to take the day off. I called the precinct and left a message. Patrolman Burke rang back after dark.

"It's the first Monday of the month," I said.

"Right. Did Pinky call?"

"Yeah, but we missed each other."

"How come?"

"I left the store closed all day."

"Good thinking, Batman."

"Tomorrow's the first Tuesday of the month," I said. "I'm expecting a visit from Montalbano's crew, remember?"

Burke covered the phone while he consulted with his partner. When he came back on the line he said, "We're on rotation. I suggest you do the same thing."

"What? Work nights?"

"Keep the store closed for the day."

I was losing the plot.

***

The next morning, I took up sentry duty in the window of the coffee-shop.

Ten o'clock on the nose, Montalbano's two hoodlums came calling. They knocked on the door of my store. They rattled the lock. Shading their eyes, they peered in through the glass. Then they went away.

I debated whether I could open the store and decided not to risk it. Which was just as well. A few minutes past eleven the two thugs were back, and again at twelve-thirty, two-fifteen, and four o'clock.

By this time my liver thought I'd joined the temperance movement. The bar owner was giving me strange looks. He came over and began wiping my table with an oily rag.

"Nice place you've got here," I said.

"Thanks. More coffee?"

"How long you had this place?"

"What's it to you?"

"Just making friendly conversation," I said, showing him my palms.

He eyed me up and down before answering. "Three years, nearly. Why?"

I said, "Do you pay insurance?"

His eyes narrowed. "Sure, I pay insurance. What you driving at, buster?"

That 'buster' told me it was time to get to the point. "I meant insurance against fires, looters, broken windows."

He turned on his heels and disappeared behind the bar. When he reappeared the business end of two barrels were pointed squarely at my midriff.

"Out!" he said, waving the gun.

I headed for the door, leaving my dignity on the table with my change.

"And don't come back," he shouted. To emphasize the point he fired one round into the air behind me.

I ran. Long legs run in our family.

***

A couple days later I smelled smoke coming from the storeroom. It was a small fire, but growing. It's what fires do best. By the time I had my fire extinguisher working it was already too big for me to handle on my own. I called the Fire Department.

It took the firemen about ten minutes to get set up and put the fire out. They even had time for a coffee break. One of them said he'd seen more flames on a good Cuban cigar. "You need insurance," he added, handing me his business card.

I read 'Poldark Fire Assurance – for the discerning small businessman'

"Can't afford it," I said.

He gave me an unreadable smile and went off to roll up his hose.

The damage to the storeroom was minimal, but about a quarter of my stock was a write-off. Unless there's a market for mulled wine and pre-smoked cigarettes that I don't know about.

Piece of crap, that fire extinguisher.

I rang the precinct.

The patrolmen arrived within fifteen. They took a look inside the storeroom.

Burke said, "They poured gas under your loading bay door."

"Who's 'they'?" I said.

Kerrigan shrugged. "No way of knowing. You should keep that door locked at all times."

"It was locked." I wondered was this the sort of expert advice I was paying my taxes for.

I rang Bubba.

"How was the hunting trip?" I said.

"Nah! Waste of a good week. There's no wildlife in them woods."

I told him what had happened.

He said, "Did you move your stock like I told ya?" I couldn't remember him telling me that, but maybe I'd forgotten.

"Move it off the premises. Keep the bare minimum in the storeroom. That way they can't hurt you."

There's other ways they can hurt me, I thought, but I kept that thought to myself. I had professional police protection, after all.

Bubba's a good friend. He found me a rental lock-up off J Street. I rented a U-Haul van and moved most of my stock. Bubba and an old sparring partner of his gave me a hand. I paid them in kind. Then I bought the biggest padlock I could find and put it on the lock-up. I must say, the new arrangement put my mind at ease.

I went back to the coffee shop. The owner's eyes narrowed and he ducked behind his counter when he saw me coming.

I held up a hand. "I'm not here to take your money. I'm new in town. I own the premises across the road. I just want to know what I should do when the gangsters come calling."

He shrugged. "How should I know?"

"Haven't they called looking for protection money?"

"No, they haven't. Now get outta my shop."

I backed out. And that was when I spotted the name of the shop: Montalbano and Scarpetta.

***

On Wednesday I opened up the store. There's only so many days I can stay closed if I want to remain in business. On the way to Jefferson and L, I swung by the lock-up to collect some stock.

If there's one thing sadder than a broken padlock it's an empty lock-up.

I rang Bubba and told him about the break-in.

"Sorry to hear that, Pete," he said. "I'll ask around, see if anyone knows anything."

***

At three o'clock the next afternoon, a tall man of considerable bulk entered the store. He looked familiar, but I couldn't place him. He wore heavy black brogues, a cheap navy-blue suit, a white shirt, and red braces, no tie. He waited until the other customers had left before locking the door and approaching the counter.

"I've seen your lock-up," he said, looking me square in the eye. "It's empty."

I gave him my best frown. He didn't look like one of Montalbano's mob, and if this was Pinky Sparrow then I was Sammie Davis Junior. And then I realized who he was. Patrolman Burke—or was it Kerrigan—unrecognizable out of uniform.

My blood pressure shot up a couple notches. "You were supposed to protect me."

"We were on rotation. Can't be everywhere all the time."

"But you will investigate the break-in, find the missing stock?"

He shook his head. "No future in that, Barney. Your stock's probably outta the state by now. What you need is protection, man." He rubbed his thumb and forefinger together in the universal symbol for cash.

"I pay my taxes."

"Sure you do, but that only pays for black-and-white drive-bys. You need proper protection, and that costs money."

It seemed everyone was in the protection game, Pinky Sparrow, the Italians, the Fire Department and now the city police. "Forget it, buster," I said.

***

Bubba rang back that evening with good news. "I have your stock—most of it, anyhow. I'll drop it by later."

Seven o'clock I opened the lock-up. Bubba drove up in a van and two of his mates got to work.

Bubba's a good friend.

About ten percent of the stock was missing, the rest was in mint condition.

I said, "How can I thank you? I thought I was going outta business."

"No need for thanks, Pete. Just cover my expenses." He handed me a bill.

There was the cost of hiring the van and the labor, $2,000 for the stock itself and a grand for something labeled 'sundries'. It came to $4,500. I wrote Bubba a check.

***

Bubba called my cell later that night.

"Pete, I been thinking," he said. I pictured him scratching his knuckles. "Mebbe me and the boys should keep an eye on your store and your lock-up. You don't want any more fires or break-ins."

"That's very generous of you," I said. "You'd have to let me pay for any expenses incurred."

"Right," said Bubba. "Watching two properties will require a rota of three men, I reckon. Double that for round-the-clock cover. Then there's logistics, like food and drink, gas and ammo." He paused. "Four thousand a week should cover it."

Bubba's a good friend.

WHAT COULD POSSIBLY GO WRONG?

Francis X. Conroy was a successful criminal boss, an evil mastermind who specialized in armed robberies and bank raids. His brother, Ignatius L. Conroy, was equally successful. His talent was laundering his brother's hard-earned, and he was very good at it. Within five years, the brothers each had elaborate mansions in upstate New York and holiday villas – Ignatius in Maryland, Francis in Maine – to rival anything owned by the innovators of Silicon Valley. They also jointly owned a Lear jet with a pilot on permanent retainer.

It was Danny 'Dumbo' Dunphy's time. A lost childhood followed by a misspent youth had molded him into a fully qualified muscleman. Ten years in the University of Hardscrabble and he graduated summa cum laude with a primary degree in the martial arts. By his mid-thirties he had postgraduate qualifications in the science of torture and weapons technology. He shaved his head and secured tenure in the 'west-side' gang of the brothers, Ignatius and Francis Conroy.

Working for the Conroy brothers earned Dumbo Dunphy a good screw, good enough for a Madison Avenue bespoke tailored 3-piece suit complete with fob watch on a gold chain. His duties mainly consisted of keeping order among the common members of the gang, the lifters and carriers, the muscle, the persuaders, the middlemen, and the fixers. Life in the gang was a gravy train for Dumbo, and as long as the train stayed on the rails, he was in clover.

The lifters and carriers were all Autonomic Units. Most were Mark 2 'Beta' Units, bought by the brothers to replace the much simpler Mark 1 Alphas. Then Xenodyne Automation announced the release of the Mark 3, incorporating a vastly improved processor providing higher cognitive functions with 'impressive heuristic capabilities.' The promotional material claimed that the Mark 3 AU "could be taught to play any musical instrument or build a pocket watch." Ignatius Conroy had other ideas.

The gang bought three Units, and Ignatius got to work teaching them the rudiments of the 'trade'. He started by teaching Gamma-317 how to drive. The exercise was an unqualified success; the android passed its driving test with flying colors.

Gamma-318 was trained as a safe-cracker by the well-known yeggman, 'fingers' Maclew. Maclew was close to retirement, his fingers arthritic, his knowledge outdated.

The third android, Gamma-319, was placed under Dumbo Dunphy's tutelage. Within six weeks, it could be relied on to handle most 'delicate' situations with appropriate brutality. Dumbo was proud of his protégé; he could even see some of his own moves in the way it functioned and many of his favorite expressions in its verbiage. "Cough up, dummy, or prepare to swallow your teeth," was one of his favorites.

When Francis X. Conroy received word through the grapevine that a cash-in-transit collection was scheduled for a high-class Manhattan jewelry store on a certain date, the brothers began to lay their plans. Armed with precise details of the transit van's route, Francis picked the ideal spot for the raid. The plan was to take control of the van, open the safe at the side of the road and drive away with the loot. They would allow no more than 15 minutes to open the safe. Ignatius put the raiding party together. Gamma-319 and Dumbo would provide the muscle. Gamma-318 would crack open the safe and Gamma-317 would drive the getaway car.

The plan was foolproof, and it had the additional benefit of being highly profitable; all but one of the gang members were androids, requiring no payment.

What could possibly go wrong?

The gang set up a roadblock at the selected spot and waited for the van. Dumbo Dunphy carried a chainsaw, Gamma-319 was armed with a shotgun. Gamma-317 and 318 waited in the car.

The armored van arrived on time and screeched to a halt at the roadblock. Gamma-319 waved the gun at the two guards and ordered them out of the cab. The two men climbed down, their hands in the air. Dumbo attacked the rear door of the van with his chainsaw, and quickly gained entry. Gamma-318 climbed aboard and went to work on the safe.

The safe remained stubbornly closed; the training that 'Fingers' Maclew had given Gamma-318 was inadequate for the task. Meanwhile, one of the guards recognized the vacant expression on the face of Gamma-319. He lowered his arms and took a step forward.

"What are you doing?" yelled the second guard.

Gamma-319 waved his shotgun at him. "Cough up, dummy, or prepare to swallow your teeth."

"Don't worry," the first guard replied, "It's not going to shoot us." He stepped closer to the android. "You're not going to shoot us, are you? Give me the gun, there's a good android."

Crouching beside Gamma-318 in the back of the van, Dumbo looked at his watch. The 15 minutes was up. He jumped down from the van. Gamma-318 followed him and they climbed into the getaway car. Gamma-319 jumped in under a hail of gunshot.

"Go!" yelled Dumbo to Gamma-317 at the wheel.

Twenty minutes later, F X Conroy received a call from Dumbo Dunphy.

"We don't have the money. I'm sorry, boss."

"What happened?"

"We couldn't open the safe. We ran out of time. And the guards disarmed our muscleman."

F X Conroy was speechless. "Where are you?" he said.

"I'm at the police station. We've all been arrested."

"How did the cops catch you? I gave you my fastest getaway car."

"The stupid android's programming wouldn't allow it to exceed the speed limit."

SUPERHERO FIREMAN

STEVIE SAT BY THE river, shivering in his short pants. He shared the quay with the ghostly statues of famine victims, braced against the icy wind, while a ship the size of a block of flats rusted away on the opposite quay. Seagulls wavered in the air crying to each other like babies, sometimes diving to sit on the water.

Stevie pulled the lunch his ma had packed for him from his schoolbag and unwrapped it. The cheese sandwich was gone in three mouthfuls, followed by the banana. A half-eaten chocolate bar emerged from his pocket and he made short work of that, scraping the melted chocolate from the silver wrapping with his teeth.

A black dinghy with two men on board came charging down the river. The dinghy had AIRSEA RESCUE painted on its side in big orange letters. The men wore donkey jackets. One sat at the motor, steering. The second man stood with his knees flexed like a circus performer on horseback, holding a length of rope tied like reins to the front of the dinghy.

A police car appeared on the quay opposite, its lights flashing, and then a big red fire engine arrived, its klaxon sounding like a big animal in pain.

There was something on the surface of the water beside the boat, something the size of a football drifting slower than the current, the water flowing around it. Stevie's heart began to race. It was the head of a woman. The scene began to make sense. The woman must have fallen into the river and she was being rescued!

When the dinghy reached the woman, it stopped and spun around, the motor holding it against the current. Then Stevie spotted a third rescuer wearing a black wet suit, climbing down a rusty ladder. When this man reached the bottom of the ladder he lowered himself into the water and swam towards the centre of the river. The current carried him towards the woman.

Along the opposite quay wall and on the bridge, crowds had gathered to watch, as the two men in the dinghy and the swimmer manhandled the woman into the dinghy. Stevie had a ringside view.

Once they had the woman in the dinghy, the two men ferried her over to the ladder while the swimmer held on to a rope on the side of the dinghy. The woman climbed the ladder, and the swimmer followed. When they reached the top, someone put a blanket around her shoulders and she was taken away in the police car, its siren wailing. The fire engine switched off its light and drove off. The crowd applauded and dispersed.

When Stevie looked for the dinghy it had vanished. The seagulls hovered and cried overhead as if nothing had happened.

"Shouldn't you be in school?"

A garda towered over Stevie, blocking out half the sunlight. Stevie's heart began to race again.

"My teacher sent me home. I'm sick."

"Where do you live?"

"Fatima Mansions."

The copper reached into his breast pocket and pulled out his notebook. "What's your name, son?"

Stevie was already on his last warning from the school. He wasn't sure what would happen if he was caught mitching again, but it meant big trouble – and not just at school. He came up with the name of a boy in his class who lived in the flats. "Ian Gambioni."

"Spell that," said the garda, licking his pencil.

A flush of panic swept over Stevie. He could just about spell his own name.

"Can I go? It's freezing."

"Okay," said the garda, tucking his notebook away. "Go straight home."

Stevie grabbed his schoolbag and ran off.

When it was safe, he doubled back, and ducked into O'Kelly's Amusements on the south quays. Slot machines lined the walls in two rooms, six players moving among them working the handles, putting in their hours like factory workers.

Stevie did the rounds checking the trays for spare change and came up with three twenty-cent coins. With the two in his pocket, that made five. It was his lucky day! He checked the machines and found one with cherries just above the centre line in the left-hand tumbler. A good strong pull should land those cherries and a pay-out of two. He put a coin in and pulled the handle. Sure enough, he got the cherries in the first position. Cherries in the second position as well gave him a pay-out of five. He punched the air. He had the special skill.

***

Two hours later, the machine had swallowed all of Stevie's winnings, and Finn's money was burning a hole in his pocket. Those cherries hovered invitingly just above the line, and he was sure he could land them again.

Half an hour after that, Stevie emerged from O'Kelly's blinking and broke, a large hole in Finn's money in his pocket. Finn would murder him for sure.

It was darker now, a thin film of mist rising from the river, the evening traffic starting to build.

He found Mike the Bike in his usual spot near the Dublin Corpo offices and offered him sixteen euros.

"What's this?" said Mike.

"That's all I've got. Give us a small bag, why can't you."

Mike gave Stevie a bag and a cross-eyed look. "You'll make up the difference the next time, yeah?" It was more of a threat than a question, but still Stevie reckoned Mike must have been sampling his own merchandise.

Before he could escape, Mike grabbed him by the shoulder. "What do you wanna be when you grow up, son?"

Without a moment's hesitation, Stevie said, "A fireman."

On the way back to the flats, he thought about his answer. He would make a great fireman. He thought about it some more. What he really wanted was to be a Superhero fireman. Okay, manipulating slot machines wasn't the best superpower for a fireman, but maybe he could develop a couple of others.

***

He stopped off at Maguires, the small newsagents and grocery shop opposite the flats. Mr Maguire was old and short-sighted. He had been behind the counter that morning, and Stevie had filched two chocolate bars. But the woman was on duty now, and she had eyes in the back of her head.

He waited until two adults went into the shop, then stepped in behind them and wandered around by the newspaper stand. Out of the corner of his eye he could see the display on the counter that held the chocolate bars. There was no way he could slip one into his pocket without being seen by the woman. His only chance was to grab a handful and make a dash for it.

"Can I get you something?" the woman said, coming out from behind the counter.

The two adults had got what they'd come for and left. Stevie's cover was blown. He looked up at her. She was doughnuts fat, with bare arms like tree trunks folded under massive breasts. Stevie knew she could read his mind.

"I'm just looking, Missus."

Her eyes were like laser death rays. "I know who you are, and I know your mother. Get out of here."

"I'm not afraid of you," he shouted as he ran out of the shop.

Ma was in her usual place on the sofa facing a blank TV screen. She lit a new cigarette from the butt of her old one. Stevie dropped his school bag on the floor and switched on the TV.

"Don't you have homework?"

"Nah. The teacher gave us a day off homework."

"Why?"

"It's Airsea Rescue Day." It was the first thing that popped into his head.

"I never heard of that. What's that about?"

"It's so people can raise money for... rescues."

His mind was full of the rescue he'd seen. He was bursting to tell his ma all about it, but how could he? He watched children's television for half an hour, and then Finn came in with his pointy shoes and two fish suppers.

He had a copy of *The Evening Herald*. When Stevie saw the headline. "WOMAN PULLED FROM LIFFEY" he had to clamp his mouth shut to stop from blurting it all out. The effort gave him a pain in his stomach.

"Fetch some plates and forks from the kitchen, love. And take this." She handed Stevie her overflowing ashtray. Ma had smoked all her life from the age of twelve. Stevie reckoned she was afraid to stop. A woman she knew from Finglas gave them up and died within a year.

Stevie emptied the ashtray and divided out the two fish suppers between the three of them, like Jesus with the loaves and the fishes.

Finn sat beside Ma on the sofa. As they tucked into their food, he read his newspaper, his ponytail bobbing about behind his bald head. "Some eejit jumped in the river. It says here the police were after her so she jumped in. Listen to this. 'The woman was taken to Blanchardstown Hospital and from there to the Bridewell Garda station for questioning.' Musta been one o' them shopfitters."

Stevie knew Finn meant 'shoplifters'. He often mixed up words. Sometimes he made mistakes, but sometimes he did it on purpose.

Ma said, "Was she all right, after?"

"Wouldn'ta thought so. Probably had a bellyful o' Liffey water."

They finished their suppers in time for the midweek lottery. Finn lined up his tickets on the arm of the sofa and cheered or groaned as each number was drawn. When the draw was over, Finn tore up his tickets in disgust.

There were pictures on the news of the woman being pulled from the river. After the news, Finn chose a channel with a rubbish football match, and Stevie fell asleep on his cushion.

A blast of cold air woke him. The front door was open and there was an enormous guard in navy blue standing in front of the telly.

Stevie froze. He couldn't tell if this was the same guard he'd met on the quays. They all looked the same. When he remembered the stash in his pocket, he said, "I'll make tea." He went into the kitchen and slipped the baggie into the oven.

Stevie made a cup of tea and handed it to the guard.

"Where were you this morning?" Ma said. "And before you start telling lies, Garda Moran says he found you on the quays."

Stevie swallowed to clear a lump in his throat.

The guard said, "You do realise giving a false name to a garda is a serious offence?"

"I was confused."

Finn snorted. "Confused about yer own name?"

"What were you doing on the quays? Why weren't you at school?" The whine in Ma's voice gave Stevie fair warning of what was to come.

"Skipping school is another serious offence," said the guard.

"The teacher sent me home," said Stevie.

Ma flicked ash from her cigarette. "I'll speak to Mrs Walsh in the morning. We'll see what she has to say about that."

When the guard had gone, Stevie took the baggie from the oven and handed it to Finn. Maybe if Finn smoked some weed Stevie could still avoid a beating. But Finn knew what he was at. He grabbed Stevie by the arm.

Stevie shouted at him. "Let me go, you bully. You're not my da."

Finn dragged him into the bathroom and removed one of his winkle-pickers. Stevie pounded Finn's chest. He shouted, "Ma, tell him to leave me alone."

***

In the cold morning, Stevie's backside was still tender. His mind was full of what had happened. He was in big trouble with Ma, Finn and his teacher. The woman in the shop could make things worse. And how was he going to make up the money he owed to Mike the Bike?

But then he laughed. He was a Superhero fireman and 'trouble' was his middle name.

THE HAPPY HOBO

Two homeless men slept behind a dumpster under the shadow of JFK Stadium. This was a desolate alley off Tenth Street, seldom visited by the city police or street cleaning crews. It was November, and the dumpster provided a measure of shelter from the bitter north wind.

At 6:00 a.m., Windy awoke with a start and got to his feet. He coughed, ran his fingers through his beard, and reached for a bottle in his coat pocket.

He was tall, well-built, but bowed. His clothes had seen better days. His coat, a threadbare woolen garment of dark gray, reached only as far as his knees. Only his boots were strong and watertight—a relic from his army days.

He lifted the bottle to his lips and took a swig.

Lonesome sat up. "Pass the bottle."

Windy snorted and took another slug.

Lonesome struggled to his feet. He was six inches taller than his companion, similarly dressed and with an identical full-length beard. He picked up his battered fedora and placed it on his head. "Share and share alike," he said.

"Yeah, right." Windy hesitated, then he handed it over.

Lonesome grabbed the bottle and emptied it down his throat—there was barely a mouthful left. He tossed the empty bottle into the dumpster.

"You were shouting in your sleep again," said Lonesome.

"What else is new?" said Windy.

***

Later, they sat together in a doorway making their plans for the coming day. Torn fragments of newspapers danced around their feet in the swirling, icy wind.

"Twenty-fi' dollars," Lonesome said.

Windy snorted. "You and whose army?"

"I'm not sleeping rough again. It was brass monkeys last night."

The conversation died while each man contemplated the eternal puzzle: how to extract enough cash from the regular people of Hoboken to pay for a drink and a night's shelter.

"What day is it?" Windy said.

"Wednesday or Thursday."

"Right. Washington Street. You take the south entrance. I'll take the north."

Before heading off toward the mall they climbed into the dumpster. They had rummaged through it the night before, but Lonesome reckoned it was worth another look. Windy pulled out a tangle of metal coat hangers, and held them up for inspection. Lonesome shook his head. Windy tossed them back. One corner of the dumpster contained plastic bags of domestic garbage. Out of this corner scurried two rats. Using Windy's boots as a shortcut and a plank as a highway, they scampered out of the dumpster. Windy swore.

"Didn't I tell you to stay outa that corner?" Lonesome said.

A minute later Windy reached down, picked something up and slipped it into his pocket. Lonesome spotted the movement immediately.

"What you got?"

"Nothin'."

"Show us what you got."

"It's nothin'. I'll show you later. Come on, we better make tracks."

***

Seamus McGuire's bar is located five blocks west of Washington Street Mall. One of the busiest bars in New Jersey, serving a wide variety of food, there is always something to be had in the alley out back. Windy arrived, just after noon, after a morning begging in the mall. Lonesome was in the line ahead of him with three other bearded drifters, two ahead and one behind him. The rear door to the kitchen was open wide, the vent in the walls spilling steam and mouthwatering smells into the alley. The hustle of the chefs and waiters could be seen through the open door, and there was a constant flow of shouted orders, accompanied by the rattle of pots and pans, plates and cutlery.

"Two nachos, one wings and a shrimp basket."

"Two soups, one special, three fries."

Happy sounds!

Lonesome surrendered his place to the man behind him to be next to his friend.

"How much you got?"

"Seven dollars and change." Lonesome looked downcast. "How about you?"

"Six bucks and a few cents."

Lonesome squinted at his friend. "I swear you scare folks with that long face."

"I smile. I smile at the kids."

"Prob'ly makes matters worse," mumbled Lonesome.

One of the short-order chefs appeared at the door holding a plate. "Salad, barely touched."

The first man took the plate and moved to the end of the line behind Windy. The next man received a plate of miserable-looking chicken nacho leftovers—mostly bones. He took the plate and moved to the end of the line.

The third man in line—now a place ahead of Lonesome—got a plate of leftover spare ribs. Barely any meat left on the bones.

Lonesome was next in line. There was a long wait before the next plate arrived. Carlos, the washer-up handed out a half-plate of cold, congealed chili.

Windy rolled his eyes. "Not much to write home about, there, Lo."

"Share and share alike," Lonesome said.

"Yeah, right."

Almost immediately, the head chef stepped into the doorway carrying a basket of chicken drumsticks and French fries. "Cancelled order. Enjoy." He handed the basket to Windy.

The food was lukewarm but there was plenty of it. The man at the end of the line glared at them and spat on the ground; he had gained a place but missed the jackpot.

Lonesome handed his plate of leftover chili to the man behind them and they moved to the end of the line together.

"Share and share alike, right, Windy?"

Windy threw him a grin.

By the time they had been around the loop once more it was close to 2:00 p.m. and their hunger had been quelled. One of the barmen came down the steps into the alley with a crate of empty bottles. Most were beer bottles, but four were wine and there was one vodka bottle. Under the envious eyes of the other three hobos, Windy and Lonesome took possession of this treasure. They went through the crate, collecting all the liquid remnants into one bottle. When they had finished they had accumulated a half pint of mixed alcohol. They shared this between them, their eyes smarting from the foul taste.

"Better get back to work," Lonesome said.

Windy tossed the empty bottle aside. "No rest for the wicked."

On the way back to the mall, Lonesome said, "What did you pick up from the dumpster this morning? You never told me."

Windy pulled a small plastic medicine bottle from his coat pocket and handed it to his friend.

Lonesome read the label. "Prozac. Take two, then one each day or as directed. What are they for?"

Windy shrugged. "Who knows."

"How many's in there?"

"I haven't counted them."

"Have you taken some?"

"I took two this morning."

"And?"

Windy shrugged again. "Nothin' so far."

Lonesome swallowed one of the pills and handed the bottle back.

They met again at 10:00 p.m. in the alley behind McGuire's. The place was alive with homeless men, most all of them drunk, many sleeping amongst the garbage cans. They joined a small group of three standing around a rusty brazier, growling at each other like horny tomcats.

"How'd you do?" Lonesome said.

"Thirteen bucks."

"Is that all? You had seven this morning."

"Yeah, but I bought a couple drinks. What you got?"

"Twelve dollars and change."

Windy held his hands over the fire. "Is that all? You had seven earlier. You spent how much?"

"I had nothin' to drink all day. God's truth."

Windy peered at his friend. Apart from occasional flurries of sparks from the brazier, the only light in the alley came from the open kitchen door. Lonesome's face was completely in shadow, but from the way he stood, the way he held his head, Windy knew his friend was lying. "Yeah, right," he said.

***

The next day they tried the Jefferson Street Mall. The day after that was Sunday; they blew all their remaining money on cheap wine. By Wednesday they were back at Washington Street Mall. Windy took the south entrance, Lonesome the north. It was a mind-numbingly beautiful day—clear blue icy skies, a light stiff breeze, birds singing, children laughing.

Windy positioned himself at the entrance to a ladies' beauty parlor. A portly, middle-aged woman with blue hair approached.

"Good morning, Madam." Windy opened the door for her with a flourish.

She stiffed him and ducked inside. The next woman to arrive was younger, or so it appeared to Windy. He greeted her, and moved ahead of her toward the door.

"Allow me, ma'am." He beamed at her.

"Thank you." She sniffed at him.

"It's no bother. No bother at all."

The woman stopped in the doorway and gave him a five from her purse. "Nice smile," she said by way of explanation.

The third woman to come along was carrying a miniature dog in a large handbag.

"Mind your pooch for you, Miss?" said Windy. His offer was rejected, but she gave him a dollar.

By mid-morning he had picked up seventeen dollars in tips, and his beaming smile was wider than ever.

A woman approached with a large, hairy German shepherd on a lead. The dog pulled on his lead, straining every sinew to escape. It reminded Windy of the wild dogs of Iraq, driven to the brink of insanity by the bombs and their hunger—the stuff of one of his recurring nightmares.

Windy tipped an imaginary hat. "Good morning, Madam. Why not let me take your dog for a walk while you're inside?"

"No thank you."

"What that dog needs is a good brisk walk. Tire him out. Make him easier to handle."

She shook her head.

"You don't trust me," he said. "That's only natural. I tell you what, I'll give you ... ten bucks as a sign of good faith." He pulled the money from his pocket and thrust it at her. "I'll walk the legs off—what's his name?"

"Napoleon."

"I'll walk the legs off of Napoleon here while you're inside, and when I return you can give me back my money plus ten for the service."

The deal was struck. Windy and Napoleon walked round and round the block at pace. After an hour, the woman emerged from the salon with a new extravagant hair-do.

She paid Windy twenty dollars, and took Napoleon's lead. "Thank you."

"Glad to be of service, Ma'am."

At the end of the day, the two men met in the alley behind McGuire's. Lonesome had seventeen dollars to show for the whole day's work. Windy had forty-seven dollars and fifty-five cents.

"Forty-seven bucks!" Lonesome whistled. "How much did you spend?"

"I had a coupla beers. I collected over sixty, I reckon."

"We have enough for the hostel for both of us."

"What you mean is: I have enough for a bed and a good meal. You've got fourteen bucks."

"Share and share alike," said Lonesome.

"Yeah right," said Windy.

***

They paid fifty dollars for two beds in the Franciscans' waterfront hostel, and in the morning, they each had a good wash. Old Brother Ambrose, in charge of the kitchen, gave them a plate of beans each for breakfast.

"We've no money," Windy said.

The friar rubbed the side of his nose. "It'll be our secret."

Back on the street, Windy said, "I wonder what came over that monk."

"You charmed him," Lonesome said. "The way you did with the ladies at the mall."

"Must be my aftershave."

The two men laughed. Windy couldn't remember the last time they'd laughed together. Maybe on the trip out to Kuwait before the shooting started. Across the river, the Manhattan skyline looked almost inviting in the rising sun.

By noon on Saturday Windy had been raking in the tips so quickly he had lost count. He had money in several pockets. By dead reckoning he thought he must have at least fifty dollars. He was dying to find a quiet corner somewhere and count his haul. When his best customer—the lady with the German shepherd—arrived, she smiled at him.

"Good afternoon, Madam. And how's Napoleon today?"

"Frisky," she said. "Give him a good run around, tire him out, and I'll give you an extra five dollars."

Windy couldn't guess at her age. Dressed in artificial fur, and heavily made up, her hair dyed blonde, the roots showing, Windy thought she would probably be attractive to many men.

"Very good, Madam."

She handed him the lead. "What's your name?"

"Michael, but everyone calls me—" He balked at his nickname. What sort of name is that? Without thinking, he blurted out the first name that came into his head, "Everyone calls me Lonesome."

"Right, Lonesome, see you in an hour."

An hour later, he handed Napoleon's lead back to his owner, and she gave him fifteen dollars.

"He looks worn out." She looked directly at Windy and laughed. "You too, Lonely."

"That's Lonesome," said Windy.

"And are you?"

"Am I what?"

"Lonesome?"

"No, I have a friend." Something about the way she looked at him then made him blush behind his beard.

His tally for the day was ninety-five dollars. Lonesome had nine dollars and forty-seven cents.

Windy said, "That's pretty miserable even by your standards, Lo."

"You took it all," Lonesome growled. "By the time they got to me, you'd stripped 'em bare."

*****

That night they paid fifty dollars up front for two beds in the hostel. Then they had a proper meal in the seaman's mission down by Pier A—beef stew with boiled potatoes followed by jelly sponge pudding in custard—six dollars each.

Windy was telling his friend about his conversation with Napoleon's mistress when they were joined at the table by two older men, called Nat and Pat. Veterans of the Vietnam War, both men were of similar build, both had long gray beards with dark streaks, and both had drooping lower eyelids, their bloody undersides exposed. Nat wore a Chicago Cubs baseball cap; Pat was bareheaded; it was the only way anyone could tell them apart.

"How old was she?" Lonesome said to Windy.

"Fortyish. Fifty maybe." Windy's tongue was busy trying to dislodge a sliver of beef from between two of his teeth.

Lonesome leered. "A looker?"

"You better believe it," Pat said.

Lonesome and Windy exchanged a glance, then they both looked at Pat; he seemed totally engrossed in his meal. It was as if he hadn't spoken.

"She was okay," Windy said.

"Did you get her name?"

"No."

"Josephine, I bet." Lonesome grinned.

"You better believe it," said Pat.

They both looked at Pat again.

Lonesome said, "What's your problem, old man?"

Pat and Nat continued shoveling food into their mouths. Neither man looked up.

"Who's Josephine?" Windy said, using his fingernail to dislodge the sliver of beef, then popping it back into his mouth.

"Napoleon's mistress," Lonesome replied.

Windy continued to look confused.

Nat and Pat left with them, and the four men walked back to Tenth Street together. They stopped off at the liquor store on the corner of Twelfth and Willow, where Windy bought three bottles of wine, two flagons of cider and a half-bottle of cheap vodka.

By three o'clock in the morning, all four men were well pickled. The hostel had closed for the night; their money was all gone. They sat side by side in a row in the alley, sharing the last flagon of cider.

"You know what you should do." Nat said to Windy.

Lonesome answered him. "What? What should he do, old man?"

"He should get hisself a geetar."

"I can't play," Windy said. "I never been musical."

"Don't take much to play a geetar. Make loadsa money with a geetar," said Nat.

"You reckon," Lonesome said.

"You better believe it," said Pat.

Later, the two older men were asleep. Lonesome said, "Any of them drugs left?"

"They're all gone."

"You been takin' them?"

"Ev'ry day, like it says on the bottle."

"And?"

"No effect. But the nightmares have eased off a bit."

***

The next week went by in a flash. Windy's takings hovered close to a hundred dollars each day. Lonesome snarled and bared his teeth at Pat and Nat from time to time, but the old men continued to hang around. Thanks to Windy's generosity, all four became regulars at the seaman's mission.

One evening after a meal of chili and rice, they stood at the waterfront, braving an arctic wind, watching the boats pass up and down the river. They were joined at the barrier by two more drifters, a young Irishman with the nickname "Galway" and an older man known as "Red."

Across the water, the lights of Manhattan mingled with the stars. Windy felt drawn to the place, as in the past. He knew that he could easily double his daily intake on the other side of the river.

He said, "Maybe ..."

"Maybe what?" said Galway.

"Maybe nothin'," said Lonesome, taking ahold of Windy's arm.

Before settling for Hoboken, Windy and Lonesome had tried their luck in New York City. Hounded out by the store owners of the Bronx, assaulted by the resident hobos of Central Park, and cold shouldered by the whores of Brooklyn Heights, they had finally found an uncontested spot on the Upper West Side, only to be moved on by New York's Finest.

Windy said, "I thought maybe ..."

"Yeah, I know," said Lonesome. "But it's not for us. Remember what happened last time. Let's go."

They headed west and then south to the corner of Eighth and Garden, where they bought a load of wine and cider. Windy paid. On leaving the liquor store they found Pat, Nat, Galway and Red waiting for them.

Lonesome put his load down and ran at them waving a fist and shouting, "Get lost." The four men retreated and then hung back as Windy and Lonesome walked on, but Windy was aware that they were still there, following a half-block behind.

***

Three hours later, Lonesome opened the last bottle of wine and handed it to Windy. Windy took a swig and passed it to Pat. Nat was next, then Red and then Galway. Galway took a long swallow, and placed the bottle between his knees.

"Pass it on," Lonesome said, glowering at him.

Galway lifted the bottle to his lips again.

Lonesome leaned across and snatched the bottle, spilling some. "Greedy bastard."

He took a swig, and offered the bottle to Windy. The bottle went round the circle again. When it got to the young Irishman, he finished it, holding the bottle upside down to show them all that it was empty.

"Greedy Irish bastard!" Lonesome shouted, jumping to his feet.

Galway and Lonesome squared off. Lonesome threw a punch, catching the younger man on the shoulder. They grappled, but while Galway was younger and fitter, Lonesome had weight, strength and military training on his side. Within two minutes Galway was on the ground, pinned under Lonesome's boot and squealing like a piglet.

"Get him off me! Let me go!"

Lonesome released him. Then Lonesome launched an attack with his fists on Red. A few of his blows caught Red about the face, and the older man fell to the ground.

After that there was a lot of yelling, and Galway and Red found a new spot a few yards down the alley.

"What about you?" Lonesome said, turning on Nat. "Don't you want to go with your buddies?"

Nat said nothing, cowering beside Pat in Windy's shadow.

That night, Nat and Pat salvaged some cardboard from the dumpster and bedded down behind it.

***

The following Monday in the mall, a small boy became separated from his parents and his sister. Windy helped to reunite him with his family, and the boy's parents offered to buy Windy a meal. He took his place at the table in McDonalds, looking like a larger-than-life uncle on a visit from the boondocks. The kids loved him; the adults laughed at his old jokes. They asked if he was in Desert Storm. He admitted that he was, and spun them a yarn built from urban myths and half-truths embellished with scenes from old, half-remembered movies. The truth was far from PG material.

After the meal, the boy's father gave Windy ten dollars and he bought a small mouthorgan from a music store. He hurried back to Tenth Street. Nat and Pat were there, nursing a bottle of cider. Windy showed them his new acquisition.

"Play something," Nat said.

"I can't. I don't know how."

"It's easy. All you got to do is blow."

Windy raised the instrument to his lips, closed his eyes and blew. It took him fifteen seconds to figure out that the mouthorgan played the even notes on blow and the odd ones on suck. With Nat's help it took a half-hour to figure out how to produce one note at a time, and by the end of the hour he could play *Michael, Row the Boat Ashore*.

The next day Nat showed him how to use his cupped hands to modulate the instrument's tone. Windy spent the night practicing, trying to play every tune that he could remember. Nat sat with him, encouraging him.

Lonesome groaned. "Can't we get a little peace?"

Three days later Windy began his new career as a street performer outside the beauty salon in Washington Street Mall. Placing an old cardboard box on the ground at his feet, he began with a double helping of *Home on the Range*, followed by *Yankee Doodle Dandy*.

His takings for that day were seventy-five dollars. And that night there were six bearded men sitting in a circle in the alley behind JFK stadium. Pat and Nat were there and so was Red; Galway had moved on and his place had been taken by 'Itchy', another Desert Storm veteran.

Itchy was an ebullient sort, given to raucous laughter. Lonesome and Windy knew him well. Lonesome was not over fond of his backslapping heartiness.

The day after that was Saturday. Windy met the woman with the dog again. She stood listening with a small crowd while he played *The Star-Spangled Banner* with gusto. When he'd finished, the woman clapped with the others, coins were tossed into his box and the crowd moved on.

The woman approached Windy; Napoleon became skittish, wagging his tail fit to burst.

She smiled at him. "You're not walking dogs these days?"

"No, Ma'am, sorry. As you can see, I've decided to try something new."

"Napoleon will miss his walks."

"You could take him out yourself," Windy said. "Big dog like that needs lotsa exercise."

He made eighty dollars that day, and the Monday after that, Lonesome took early retirement.

"Aint you goin' to work?" Windy asked.

"Can't see the point."

"Whatcha mean?"

"What's the point of me workin' my butt off for a few dollars each day? You earn enough for the both of us."

"You're a lazy bastard, Lonesome."

"You better believe it," said Lonesome.

Perhaps sensing the storm that was to come, Nat and Pat kept quiet, avoiding eye contact with either of the other two.

"What's your next move?" Lonesome said.

Windy shrugged. "I figured I'd try a few more tunes. I only got four."

Nat looked up, opening his mouth to speak.

"What you lookin' at?" Windy shouted at him.

Lonesome said, "Leave him be. I bet he's got a few more songs he could teach ya."

Nat closed his mouth again and turned his head away

"Hey Nat, don't you think it's time you was movin' on?" Windy stood over him. "What you got to say for yourself? Cat got your tongue, old man?"

Again, Lonesome said, "Leave him be, Windy."

***

Early in December, Windy was interviewed in the mall by a reporter from a local newspaper. The following day Windy's smiling face appeared in the newspaper accompanied by a feature article under the headline: "The Happy Hobo of Hoboken."

Nat read some of it out loud. "It says here, 'Lonesome has been living on our streets for the past ten years.'"

"Has it really been that long?" Windy said.

"Never mind about that," Lonesome said. "How come they got our names mixed up?"

"Sorry about that, Lo. I figured ..."

"What?"

"I figured you wouldn't mind."

They passed the flagon around a few times, before Lonesome spoke again. "I forgive you."

Windy put the flagon down between his knees. "What you saying, Lo?"

"I'm saying, you're my buddy. I forgive you for stealing my handle. Never give it another thought. Water under the bridge."

***

The morning of December 9, the day of the Jets' last game of the season, Windy announced his intention to play the entrance to Meadowlands Stadium.

"Should be worth a hundred bucks," he said.

"You better believe it. Could be more," Pat said garrulously.

"I need someone to collect the moolah," Windy said, looking at Lonesome.

Lonesome gave no answer. He stared back at Windy like he was a stranger.

"All you gotta do is hold out your hat," Windy said.

"It's a long walk," Lonesome said.

"Coupla hours. We leave now we'll make it in time. Easy."

"Nat can do it," Lonesome said.

"You'd do it better," Windy said. "Nat's too old."

"Nat'll do fine." Lonesome waved an arm. The discussion was over.

They arrived at Meadowlands early. Lines were beginning to form at the turnstiles. The crowd was noisy, keyed up, many outfitted in their team's colors: Red for the Bears, green for the Jets. Windy played his six tunes up one line and down the next, while Nat collected small change in his cap.

They had just started on the third line, when a uniformed cop approached.

"Move along. You can't play that here," he said, the heel of his hand resting on the butt of his gun in its holster.

Nat and Windy scuttled off round the side of the stadium.

"How much we got?" Windy asked.

Nat lowered himself to his knees, collected his takings into a pile and counted it.

"Sixty-four dollars, give or take," he said, grinning.

"That's not bad for thirty minutes work."

"Let's go," said Nat. They had passed a liquor store two blocks back toward Tenth Street.

Windy shook his head. "Give me half, and I'll see you later."

"What're you gonna do?"

"Watch the game."

Nat jammed his cap on and headed off alone. Windy joined one of the lines at the front of the stadium.

***

The strains of *Anchors Aweigh* echoed around the stadium. Dressed in their magnificent green and black uniforms, the band marched in formation up and down the field in full flow. There was a good crowd, most in their places, the latecomers finding their way to their seats. Windy had to be careful to avoid the young kids rushing about on last-minute errands.

Fox had supplied a battery of cameras to record the game for later transmission, and Windy found a corner seat close to one of these.

The band came to a halt at the 50-yard line. Squinting into the sun, Windy found it difficult to see; he watched pictures of the musicians as they appeared on the giant screen at the end of the stadium. Suddenly, he was looking at his own image. People were pointing and he heard folks near him say, "That's the hobo. That's Lonesome, the happy hobo of Hoboken." Windy waved at the camera. His smiling image waved at the crowd and many in the crowd waved back. Then everyone stood to attention as the band played *The Star-Spangled Banner*.

After the national anthem, the crowd cheered, the band dispersed, and the two teams ran onto the field.

The next Monday, Windy's photograph reappeared on the sports page of the newspaper beside the headline "Hoboken's Happy Hobo Fails to Lift the Jets", and the sub-title "Chicago Bears Wipe Out Jets 46-3."

In the mall, he saw many smiling faces. It was as if he had been adopted by every family in town. Young kids spoke to him; people called him "Lonesome" and everyone gave him money, even between tunes.

His take that day was close to $200.

***

He made $170 on Tuesday, and then on Wednesday he moved to Jefferson Street Mall, where he was joined by Nat. Windy played his mouthorgan, and Nat joined in, beating out the rhythm on a couple of old spoons. They were like a small combo. One kid laughed and called them "ZZ-Top."

At the end of the day they met up with Lonesome and Pat on Pier-A.

"How'd you get on?" Lonesome asked Windy.

"Three hundred and thirty-two dollars," said Windy.

"And fifty-three cents," said Nat.

"Could be a world's record," Lonesome said.

"You better believe it," said Pat.

They ate like kings.

They bought a load of drink—cider and hard liquor—and returned to their base in Tenth Street, where they found Itchy and Red waiting for them. It was a dark night, a crescent moon ducking behind thick broken cloud. Pat lit a small fire using wood from the dumpster. After a couple hours serious drinking, another two old drifters arrived, and an hour after that there was one more; word of Windy's success had gotten around. Now there were nine bearded men around the fire and a flagon of cider barely made it once around the circle. Itchy told a story from Desert Storm and Nat trumped it with a hair-raiser from his time in Nam.

"Play us a tune," Itchy said, and Windy played his latest tune *The Lonesome Cowboy*, accompanied by Nat on the spoons.

Lonesome relieved himself behind the dumpster, close to where Nat and Pat had been sleeping. Then Red sang. Nobody recognized the song, but it made Red weep.

Later, when most of the older men had fallen asleep, Lonesome said, "It's time I moved on."

Windy made no reply.

"D'ya hear me?" Lonesome raised his voice.

There was a long pause before Windy answered. "I hear you. Where you goin' to move to?"

"South."

Another long pause.

"We're doin' all right here," Windy said. "What makes you think we could do any better down south?"

"It's too focken cold here."

Windy threw another plank onto the fire. Sparks flew. The fire spat and hissed, and spat again.

"If you do go," Windy said, "you'll go on yer own."

A full minute went by before Lonesome answered. "Yeah, I know."

Windy couldn't remember the last time they'd argued. Maybe out in Kuwait, the night when the killing started.

***

When Windy woke, a burly police officer was shaking him by the shoulder.

Windy gained his feet and looked about him. There were red and blue flashing lights—an ambulance, two police cars. The sun was low in the sky. A small crowd had gathered at the end of the alley.

"Your name?" the first policeman said, as he secured Windy's hands behind him with a pair of handcuffs.

"Michael. My name's Michael Daly, but everyone calls me—"

"Yeah, yeah, we know. Why did you kill him, Lonesome?"

"Kill who?"

"Your friend."

"I never …"

"We got a witness." the policeman looked grim-faced.

Windy shook his head. "I never killed nobody."

"Like I said, we got a witness."

"Who?"

"Lady with a dog. She spoke to Nat before he died. He named his killer."

"He named me?"

"Yup. Clear as day. He said 'Lonesome did it.'"

Windy looked around for Lonesome, but he was gone.

"I'm Lonesome," Itchy said in a loud, clear voice, stepping forward.

Red stood up. "I'm Lonesome," he said.

Two more drifters got to their feet, shakily.

"I'm Lonesome," said one.

"Me too," said the other one.

The two officers exchanged a look.

Then Pat stepped forward.

"Don't tell me," the first officer said. "Your name is Lonesome."

"You better believe it," said Pat.

RETRIBUTION

MARIO MET THE NURSE at the door and took the handles of the wheelchair from her. Wrapped in a tartan blanket in the chair sat a withered old man doing a convincing impersonation of one of Snow White's small companions. Grumpy.

"How's he been?" Mario said.

"Your father's been as cantankerous as ever," the nurse replied. "But we all love him just the same. Isn't that right Mr. Gambioni?" She smiled at the old man, tucking the blanket around his legs.

Gambioni scowled, grinding his dentures.

The nurse produced a small bag of bread from a pouch in her uniform. Mario took it from her and she returned to her duties indoors.

"How are you, Pop?" Mario said

"How do I look?"

Mario knew better than to answer a question like that. Tipping the chair back to lift the front wheels from the gravel, he pushed the old man down the garden path toward the lake. It was a perfect autumn night, unseasonably warm with a brisk breeze, the lawn dressed in a scattering of large leaves, the dense shrubbery alive with color in the moonlight.

"Take it easy," said the old man. "Turn left, go left."

"Don't you want to feed the ducks?"

"Fuck the ducks. Take me to the summerhouse."

Mario pushed the chair to the left onto the lawn. As they headed toward the summerhouse, the wind tossed Mario's unruly blonde hair across his face, and he paused to sweep it from his eyes.

A haven for smokers, the summerhouse was equipped with a circular table marked with hundreds of scorch marks where the staff had stubbed out their cigarettes over many years. Mario parked the chair, engaged the brake and sat facing the old man.

Gambioni took a moment to gather the blanket around him before fixing Mario with his watery eyes. "I want you to do one last job for me," he said.

"Pop—"

"Don't interrupt me. I'm old, I'm nearly done, and I've given this a lot of thought. I'm not long for this world, son, and I won't be sorry to leave it."

Mario shook his head. "I wish you wouldn't talk like that, Pop. I'm sure you'll live for many more years."

Gambioni's eyes narrowed. "Can you imagine what it's like living like this, stuck in a chair, nothing working below the waist, pissing through a tube, not able to take a dump without help? Have you any idea the pain I've had to endure? From the moment that bullet struck my spine I was condemned to a life of agony."

"You could have been killed," Mario said.

"And it would have been better if I had. The nights I've lain in my bed wishing that they'd given the job to someone competent. If the bullet had struck an inch either side of my spine or at a slightly different angle, I wouldn't have had to suffer all those years of pain."

Mario lifted an eyebrow. "You don't know what you're saying, Pop."

Gambioni bared his dentures at Mario. "I know exactly what I'm saying. There's not a day passes that I don't pray to God for deliverance."

"What d'you want me to do?"

"Isn't it obvious? I have to draw you a picture?" He waved his long bony fingers in the air.

"You want me to help you ... to die?" Mario said.

"No, no. What are you, a retard? I want you to find the cross-eyed sonofabitch that put me in this chair." His sudden animation released a string of spittle from his mouth.

"And?"

"And I want you to do what you do best and get me payback. Closure, isn't that what they call it nowadays?"

"Retribution."

"Right. Find the bastard and kill him. If you do that I'll die happy."

Mario moistened a fingertip and began to join the scorch marks on the table, like the child's game. "We couldn't find the shooter at the time, what makes you think we could find him now?"

"Use your brain. Put the word out, offer a reward. Someone must know who did this to me."

"I don't know, Pop. Who's gonna remember? You've been out of the game for a long time."

The old man turned his head sideways to fix Mario with his gaze. "You're worried about your fee, is that it? Don't worry about that, son. You scrub the bastard, I'll double your usual fee."

Mario took a couple of moments to consider the old man's request. Then he shrugged. "Okay, Pop, I'll put one of the team on it. Eddie or Leo, maybe."

Almost imperceptibly, the old man's color deepened. On his forehead a vein began to throb. "Did I ask Eddie or Leo?" His voice trembled with something that Mario recognized—a vestige of that infamous temper that had terrorized everyone around him for years.

Mario waited for the old man to regain his composure before replying, "Why me?"

"This is personal, and you're the only one I can trust."

"And you trust me because?"

"Because you're my son. And I trust you because you're the best damn shot in the country. If you had pulled that trigger I'd have been feeding worms for the past twelve years. And besides, you owe me."

"For what?"

"I taught you everything. The business."

"You gave me my first gun. I owe you for that." Resting on the table top, Mario's hand curled into a fist. "But what else do I owe you for? Let's see. There was the daily beatings you gave me as a kid."

"You were outta control."

"At five?"

"You turned out okay. You needed discipline."

Mario continued in a steady monotone. "You treated both of us like something you'd picked up on your shoe—Mama and me—for fifteen years. I suppose I owe you for that."

"Maybe I made some mistakes—"

"And I owe you for driving her to an early grave."

Mario pulled his wallet from an inside pocket and drew out a dog-eared photograph of two people. He handed the picture to Gambioni. The old man stared at the picture through clouded eyes, his mouth clamped shut. The man in the photo had a shock of blonde hair just like Mario's. That and the square chin were dead giveaways.

Mario said, "That's Mama with Bennie Anderssen." Gambioni shook his head, and Mario continued in the same steady voice, "Don't remember him? Well, you should. You had him killed when I was two."

Gambioni looked away.

"Look at the light in her eyes. She worshipped him and you snuffed him out."

The old man whispered something.

"What was that?"

"It was just business," Gambioni mumbled.

Mario snatched the picture back. "Business? No, it was personal. It was retribution."

The old man ran a sleeve across his eyes. "After I got shot, I gave you the whole ball of wax, Mario."

Mario's eyes glazed over. His gaze drifted above the old man's head to where he'd parked the ice cream van. "You lost control long before that, old man. And you never gave me nothing, I took it from you."

"What are you saying?"

"I took it all. I was running the business for two years before I took you out."

"You ... you took me ... out?" Gambioni sucked his cheeks in, drew his lips back from his dentures, now little more than a grimacing skull.

Mario shrugged. "It was just business. But you're right, I am the best damn marksman in the world. Who else could have made that shot?"

There were tears in the old man's eyes.

Mario said, "Don't start blubbering, old man." He stood up. "I'll take you back."

"Wait, Mario. I need to say something."

Mario disengaged the brake on the wheelchair. "It's far too late for apologies."

Gambioni shook his head. "You know how much I loved you." Mario started to laugh. The old man waved a bony hand and continued, "I raised you as if you were my own. Sure, I had Anderssen scrubbed, but I was young. I'd only been married ten years. It was a terrible shock to discover that your mother had been unfaithful to me."

"You could have divorced her."

Gambioni lifted a bony shoulder.

"You must have known I'd find out."

"I swore everyone to secrecy, destroyed every picture of Anderssen that she had--"

"You missed one."

Gambioni nodded. "I knew the shooter had to be someone close, and I suspected you for years, but I needed a confession."

Mario reacted to these last words as if he'd been struck by a bullet. He cast his gaze around. All he could see was trees and thick shrubbery—ideal cover for a sniper.

"If you look closely you'll see a small microphone in the roof of the summerhouse," Gambioni said. "In a few seconds this sorry tale will be over."

"What ... what do you want from me, Pop?" Mario said, wide-eyed.

"I told you, son. Retribution."

A red sniper spot appeared on Mario's chest. He held up his hands and called out, "Whoa! Hold your fire. I can offer you much more than this old man can." He grabbed the handles of the chair and pushed it toward the sniper. "Shoot the old man, I'll give you twice what he's paying you." The red spot on Mario's chest wavered. "You can work for me. I'll make you wealthy."

"Finish the job I paid you for," Gambioni shouted from wheezing lungs.

"What can this old man offer you? He'll be dead soon. Shoot him. You owe him nothing."

The red spot shifted from Mario's chest to Gambioni's. The old man screamed, swiping at the laser spot with his hands. "You're honor bound to complete the contract. Shoot the b—"

A high-powered rifle bullet ripped through the old man's chest, killing him instantly.

Mario was not so fortunate; the bullet continued through the back of the chair, tearing into his leg near the groin, severing his femoral artery. It took him fifteen minutes to bleed out.

He died screaming.

A PATHOLOGICAL LIAR

THE BODY LAY IN a pool of blood, Dr Quinn, Medical Examiner, crouched over it.

His knees cracked as he stood up. He put his hands on his hips and stretched his back. "I'm getting too old for this."

"You and me both," said Lieutenant Lattimer. "What've we got?"

"He was a self-employed accountant. Name of Henry Cook. Went to meet his maker less than an hour ago. How did you get here so quick?"

"Nine-one-one call from a nosy neighbor. What about the cause of death?"

"I'll go with the dagger between his ribs for now, Lieutenant, unless you got a better idea."

Lattimer ignored the barb. "Anything else you can tell me about the victim?"

"Someone should probably cancel his book club membership."

"Do you have anything on the killer?"

"Whoever he is, the angle of the stab wound tells me he's right-handed ..." said Dr Quinn, filling his pipe. "... A non-smoker ..."

Lattimer pulled out a notebook and made notes.

"... 40-50 years old ..."

"How can you tell?"

"That's just an inspired guess. A younger man would have left the weapon ... Lives with his mother."

Lattimer stopped writing. "You're jerking my chain."

The doctor lit his pipe and puffed on it. "Not at all. It's classic profiling. Criminology 101." He nodded to his two aides in green coveralls. Lattimer stood aside while they lifted the body into a body bag and zipped it up. Five left the scene, only four under their own steam.

Lattimer checked the front door. There was no sign of forced entry.

Even without the dead guy the room had the look of a funeral parlor, self-assembly chipboard furniture, cheap porcelain figurines gathering dust on the mantel, nothing out of place, no sign of a struggle.

There was a file cabinet containing a load of cobwebs. Cook had precious few clients. Lattimer went through the files and came across a familiar name: Dr Quinn.

A quick check of Quinn's file produced nothing of interest.

A phone call to the precinct confirmed that Cook had no known criminal associations.

Lattimer interviewed Mrs. Cook. She was out of the house when her husband was killed. Could she think of anyone who might wanted to kill her husband? Was anything stolen? Did he owe money to anyone? All her answers were negative. Who was the last person to see him alive? One of his clients, she didn't know who.

For such a good looker, she was a poor liar.

Lattimer drove to the morgue. Dr Quinn was up to his elbows in his accountant's vital organs.

"What can I do for you, Lieutenant?" he said, hefting Cook's liver in his left hand.

"Tell me why you killed Cook."

Quinn did a double take. "What gave you that idea?"

"Several things. First, he was your accountant. You never mentioned that at the house."

"That's a bit thin, even for you," said the doctor.

"Then there was all that bullshit about the unsub: 40-50, right-handed, non-smoker living with his mother. You're in your thirties, you live alone, smoke a pipe and you're left-handed. What you gave me was a diametrically opposite profile."

The pathologist turned his attention back to the corpse.

"What was it, Doc? I know he was broke. Was he black-mailing you?"

The doctor snorted.

"Or maybe you were having an affair with his wife."

"You're clutching at straws," said the doctor, but Lattimer saw the tell in his eyes.

"Okay, explain to me how you got to the scene before I did."

JELLY BABIES

First published in Noir Nation 1, 2013

It was not raining.

Rod in hand I sat, staring at my line, limp and motionless on the silky water.

The dead surface of the canal reflected a truculent sky.

It was cold.

I prayed for rain. Rain to break the spell. Rain to warm the water and tempt the insects out of their slumber and the fish to feed.

If there were any fish.

I read a book once. It was about fishing. Fishing is all about psychology. The angler pits his wits against the fish. The fish has a strong instinct to feed but he has another stronger instinct for self-preservation. To catch a fish you have to outsmart him. First you have to choose the right bait, then you have to fool him into taking it, to persuade him to give in to his feeding instinct in spite of his instinct for survival.

Nothing moved. No breeze tickled the reeds. Even the black-windowed factory opposite lacked its usual emissions of casual steam.

That's one good thing about prison - you get lots of time to catch up on your reading. Not that I like reading. And now that I'm out, I hate books. I wouldn't read one to save my life. They just remind me of prison.

A million unwelcome memories flooded my mind as they did - as they do - every day. Deeper than the pit of hell, the mental scars of long term incarceration are for ever. Memories of personal violence, institutionalized violence, petty ritualistic power games, dehumanizing daily routines. And the endless repetitions of old black and white Bogart films, We're no Angels, The Maltese Falcon and of course, Casablanca.

Play it, Sam. Play 'As Time Goes By.'

That's another thing I hate – the cinema.

I thought about a sandwich but I was beached mid-way between breakfast and lunch, so I reached into my coat pocket, took out my bag of jelly babies, and popped one into my mouth.

... However much you feel for the little girl and her mother, you must not judge my client except on the evidence presented to you by the prosecution. Whatever crimes he may have committed in the past, he is not on trial today for those. Your job is to decide whether this man killed this little girl. And you must decide solely on the evidence presented to you by the prosecution.

An insect flew by. Another appeared, skating on the water. The reeds stirred. A light breeze ran a fingertip over the scene. A lone mongrel trotted past on the towpath. I watched him scurry about in the long grass at the side of the towpath and at the water's edge, totally at home in my presence or maybe unaware of my existence.

... If you believe, as I do, that the prosecution's case is built almost entirely on circumstantial evidence ...

Almost entirely. That was the problem, of course. That one word *almost* so nearly got me life. The video evidence was fairly damning, but a little too blurred for a definite identification. And then there was the skipping rope in the lane behind my house and the sighting of my blue van near the woods ...

My fishing line quivered and straightened lazily. Ripples appeared on the oily surface of the water catching the meager light and reflecting it in rainbow colors.

... You must ask yourselves, members of the jury, where is the prosecution's evidence? Where is the weapon, where the blood-stained clothes and where is the body?

Now, I could see the girl's mother screaming at me from across the courtroom.

The newspapers had me crucified long before the jury was sworn in. For days, the papers demanded to know why the local people were not informed that a convicted pedophile was living amongst them. They were so sure that the police had the right man. I'm not perfect, I know that. But I served my time. I paid my debt to society. And whatever happened to *innocent until proven guilty*?

Light was ebbing away into early evening. The breeze was stiffer now, worrying the reeds, and colder.

The dog began to bark. I ignored it. The barking continued, growing louder, more frenetic. Stupid mutt had found something in the water. I ignored him for a while longer, but he became more and more agitated, hysterical, until I had to go and see what all the fuss was about.

It was a black plastic bag floating among the reeds and carrying a bulky load, about three feet long. My blood ran cold at the sight. I cursed my luck.

The towpath was deserted, but there'd be people on it soon – people walking and cycling, some with dogs, children heading home from school. I leaned out and pushed the bag with my foot, but it was snagged by the reeds and just rolled lazily in the water. The dog continued to bark. I kicked out at him, catching him full in the ribs. He yelped, gave me a mournful look, and ran off. I pushed at the plastic bag again, harder this time, and slipped. Now I was standing up to my knees in the canal with the black shrouded load in my arms.

I freed it from the reeds and waded out towards the centre of the canal, pushing it ahead of me. It was heavy going against the push of the water, and each step took me deeper.

"Here, let me help you."

A young man jumped into the canal, waded through the water and stood beside me.

Together, we drew the bag back to the reeds. By the time we had lifted it on to the bank, I was exhausted and the young man had to help me climb out of the water.

"Looks too big for a litter of cats," he said. "You wait here. I'll call the police."

He ran off and I was alone with the bag. It was just about possible to make out the shape of a small body bent over in an arc inside the bag. I could see the outline of the head, the rump, an elbow, the knees and the feet. There were one or two other lumps which didn't correspond with the human form, but I guessed there were other things inside: the weapon, maybe, and bloodstained clothing.

I thought about running away, but I couldn't. It seemed I was paralyzed by my own destiny.

Life is like fishing. There's no difference, really. Children are just like small fish battling with conflicting instincts. Sometimes they run away and survive; sometimes they take the bait. The trick is to choose the right bait.

I popped another jelly baby into my mouth. Then I sat on the bank and waited for the police.

***

It was half an hour before the constable arrived. He parked his bicycle by the wall, took out his notebook and pencil and began to write.

After an age he said, "What have you been up to now, Cashman?"

I said, "This has nothing to do with me, Constable. I just found it. In the canal."

"This plastic bag?"

"Yes."

"And it has nothing to do with you, you say."

"That's right. I saw it in the water and pulled it out onto the bank."

"And have you looked inside?"

I shook my head.

"Right," he said, "let's take a look, shall we?"

He produced a small penknife and split open the bag and out fell a pile of soggy old books. No weapons, no items of clothing, and no body. Just books.

After the constable had gone, the rain came. It was no more than a drizzle, but it was enough.

WRONG NUMBER

Ben Stone sat at his desk in downtown Manchester. At least that's how Ben liked to describe the seedy suburb where his business had most recently come to rest. For the third month in a row the rent was overdue; persuading his landlord to wait another month was going to be like trying to eat black forest gateau without chocolate sauce.

Business was bad. Business was non-existent, and it had been that way for several weeks. The telephone on his desk was impersonating a black lizard basking under a desert sun. When it rang, Ben was not surprised—startled, but not surprised. Something always turns up.

"Ben Stone Investigations."

There was no response, just the sound of somebody breathing. A tingling sensation ran from the back of Ben's neck to his temples. These were the familiar goose-bumps of impending greenbacks mingled with the frisson of a free-flowing expense account.

"Who's calling?" No answer. Just heavy breathing. Harsh and rasping, it didn't sound in the best of health.

He listened to the breathing for a moment or two, and had decided to put the receiver down, when a strange, strangled voice said, "Alan Dempsey ..."

The breathing gurgled and stopped. There was a deathly silence on the line. Ben knew that his new potential client had just died. Not that he had much—any— experience with that sort of thing. He looked at the receiver in his hand. It came to him that the telephone line was the only connection he had to his caller. If he put the telephone down he could wave goodbye to any fee and that expense account.

He put the receiver to his ear again. "Hello?" There was nothing but silence on the line. Then the connection was broken.

He dialled 999.

"Emergency. Which service? Ambulance, Fire or Police?"

"Police."

"Hold on, caller. Putting you through."

"Hello, this is Manchester police emergency dispatch. Can I have your name."

"My name is Ben Stone. I want to report a death."

"A death? An accident?"

"I'm not sure."

"Okay, Mr. Stone, where are you calling from?"

"I'm calling from my office, but this is not where the death occurred."

"Where did the death occur?"

"I don't know."

The policeman took a deep breath and started again. "You wish to report a death, sir, but you don't know where it happened?"

"Yes."

"Well, what can you tell us about it?"

"I got a call from somebody. And, he ... died."

"Your caller died?"

"Yes."

"How do you know he died?"

"I just know. He gurgled and stopped breathing."

"Gurgled."

"Yes, and stopped breathing."

"And you don't know where he was calling from?"

"Afraid not."

"So how can we locate this dead caller, caller?"

"I don't know. I don't think you can."

"Right, Mr. Stone. I'll send somebody round. Give me your current location."

It was close to eleven o'clock. Ben slipped out to the patisserie across the road and bought a couple of Danish pastries before returning to his office.

***

Inspector Hackett stood over the desk, glowering at Ben. The inspector was a tall man, twenty-odd years younger than Ben, and seventy pounds lighter.

"I got this call," said Ben. "I answered it. There was a breather on the line. He sounded ill ..."

"Your caller was a man?"

"Yes, definitely a man."

"Right, go on."

"He said 'Alan Dempsey', then gurgled and stopped breathing."

"Nothing else? He said nothing else?"

"Not a dickey bird."

"So who's Alan Dempsey?"

"I don't know."

"And you have no idea who your caller was?"

"No. Maybe he got a wrong number."

"How can you be sure he died?"

"I'm pretty sure he died."

Inspector Hackett took a quick tour of the small office before returning to his original position. "You operate as a private investigator?"

"Yes. I specialize in domestic cases."

"You mean divorce cases?"

"That sort of thing, yes."

"What cases are you involved in at the moment?"

"Business has been a bit slow," said Ben.

The inspector frowned. "If this dead person rings back, call me." He placed a card on the desk. "And if I find you've been wasting police time, I'll have your license."

Ben succumbed to a black gloom. He closed the office and went to lunch in the Horse's Head. After a generous plate of Beef Bourguignon he began to feel a whole lot better. He followed this with a generous slice of lemon meringue pie and a cup of coffee, and his usual good humour was restored.

***

The following day Ben was just about to close the office and go to lunch when the telephone rang again.

"Ben Stone Investigations."

"Stone? Is that you?" It was Inspector Hackett.

"What can I do for you, Inspector?"

"We seem to have found your mystery caller. And you were right. He is dead."

"How do you know?"

"I'm a police officer."

"How do you know he is my mystery caller?"

"I pressed 'redial' on his phone."

"Who is he?"

"His name's Mike Callan. Ring any bells?"

"Never heard of him. How did he die?"

"A bullet wound to the chest from very close range. It looks like suicide."

Ben winced. "Nasty. Any idea why he wanted to talk to me?"

"Perhaps he wanted a divorce."

He found Mike Callan's address in the local telephone directory. He was listed as a pensions and investment consultant.

***

He waited three days before driving around to Mike Callan's address. The house was an opulent double-fronted 2-storey in Manor Drive, bordered on both sides by privet hedges twelve feet high. He sat in his car for a while and watched the house. There was no sign of the police and no movement into or out of the house. It looked deserted.

Ben used a skeleton key to gain entry through the back door. The house was dark inside. It smelled of air-freshener. He stood still and listened for sounds. There were none. He checked the dining room at the back of the house. There was a large bookcase full of paperbacks, and an antique roller-top desk, firmly locked.

Upstairs there were five large bedrooms, only two of which were in use. In one of these he found the chalk outline of the body and bloodstains on the mattress and the carpet by the bed. There was a telephone on the bedside table. The wardrobe was full of men's clothing.

He went back downstairs. The kitchen was a large, airy room, well designed and well equipped. He went through the contents of the refrigerator with meticulous care. It was well stocked with fresh dairy products, vegetables and German bottled beer. He checked the contents of several Tupperware containers. There was sliced chicken, fresh prawns, coleslaw.

Taped to the underside of the coleslaw container he found a locker key. He slipped it into his pocket, put everything back where he had found it and returned to the roller-top desk. The lock wouldn't budge. He was about to force it when he heard a car draw up outside.

He scurried to the back door and slipped out into the garden. As he watched, a middle-aged woman and a younger man entered the house. Ben returned to his car and waited five minutes before making his way to the front door. He rang the doorbell.

The woman opened the door. She was barefoot. He caught a glimpse of a black negligee under her housecoat.

"Mrs. Callan?"

"Yes?" She looked puzzled.

"Ben Stone, private investigator." He handed her his business card. "You don't know me, but I think we should talk. Your husband rang me on the day he died ..."

She stared at his card blankly, then she shook her head and closed the door in his face.

***

He found his landlord, John Bannister, waiting for him back at the office.

"Hi John, I suppose you've come for the rent." Ben avoided his eyes.

"You owe me three months," said Bannister.

Ben flashed his most winning smile. "I haven't got it yet, John. It's a quiet time of the year."

"With you, it's always a quiet time of the year. I'm sorry, Ben, but I'm going to have to ask you to leave. I have bills of my own that need paying."

"But I have a new client. Just give me a couple of weeks and you will be paid."

Bannister elaborated some more on his landlordly woes, but Ben knew he would agree to wait.

When Bannister had left, Ben rang Fiona Flood. Fiona worked as a salesperson for a national book publisher. She carried out surveillance work for Ben on a casual basis from time to time. He told her he had a new client.

"Who is it?"

"His name's Mike Callan."

Fiona laughed. "The investment consultant?"

"That's the guy."

"Haven't you seen the papers? He's dead. He shot himself. A client who's not breathing is a new twist, even for you."

"Nobody's perfect."

***

Day 6. Fiona arrived at ten minutes to eleven. Ben gave her tea and one of his sticky doughnuts.

She said, "Why are you fishing around this dead guy, Ben?"

"Well, he did ring me, so I suppose he wanted my help."

"Yes, maybe so, but you've no idea what he wanted, and your fee looks a bit uncertain."

"I have nothing else on the books at the moment, so why not. Maybe someone might be happy to pay up if we find his murderer."

Fiona stared at him. "I thought he topped himself."

"I'm not sure that he did," replied Ben through a mouthful of doughnut.

She raised an eyebrow. "The police seem happy enough."

"Well, I'm not. A few moments after this guy popped his clogs someone replaced the receiver."

"You're sure he was dead before you lost the line?"

"Positive."

"So you reckon there was someone else in the room with him?"

Ben dunked a second doughnut in his coffee. "I reckon so. Then there's the grieving widow and her boyfriend."

"That does sound suspicious."

Ben showed Fiona the locker key.

"Where did you find this?"

"In the fridge. Under a tub of coleslaw."

"What were you doing poking around in the fridge? No need to answer that." She grinned. "Do you want me to check this out?"

Ben nodded. "Yes. And see if you can find out whether he left a note."

***

The next day, he went to the library and read all the newspaper reports on the case. Mike Callan was investment consultant to the rich and famous. A man of legendary charisma and a flamboyant life-style, he and his business partner, Axel Greenway, had been responsible for investing an estimated two hundred million pounds of other people's money, and—it was rumoured—as much again in undeclared income.

The serious fraud squad had moved in to Callan's office to check the state of his financial dealings, and while their investigations had not yet come to a conclusion, the newspapers were already anticipating the worst. Some of his illustrious clientele and one or two of his elderly customers had broken cover to express their fears.

Alison Callan, his widow, was not directly involved in her late husband's businesses, but she had made a number of statements to the press designed to calm peoples' fears and to maintain confidence in the Callan business enterprise.

One newspaper report included an interview with a Mr. Aidan Dempsey, an irate customer of one of Callan's companies.

Ben went home. There was a note from his daughter in the letterbox: 'Ring me.'

He dialled her number.

"Hi Dad. Thanks for calling. I tried to ring you this afternoon, but I expect you were working."

"I was doing some research in the library. Is everything okay?"

"Everything's fine, Dad. Charlie sends his regards. I was wondering if you'd like to spend Christmas with us. Why don't you come for the meal and stay overnight, if you like?"

"Okay, Lucy. I'd love to. Thanks for asking. It's just as well you reminded me. I'd forgotten all about Christmas."

"Silly Daddy. Your head's always full of other people's marital problems. I'll be in your area again tomorrow. I'll drop in."

Ben threw a chicken tandoori into the microwave and opened a bottle of Chianti.

***

The following morning, day 8, Ben arrived at the office late and took a couple of Alka-Seltzers. Fiona called in at eleven. He put the kettle on. "Any luck with the locker key?"

"Of course. When have I ever let you down?" She produced a sports holdall from its hiding place beside Ben's desk. "I found this in Callan's locker at the tennis club."

"What's in it?"

"Take a look." Fiona was grinning ear to ear.

Ben unzipped the bag. It was full of smelly, unwashed tennis clothes. He recoiled, zipping it closed again, quickly. "Very funny," he said. "What about the suicide note?"

"Sorry to throw cold water on your theories, Ben, but there was a suicide note, written in Mike Callan's own hand."

Ben scratched his bald patch. "And the gun?"

"A German Luger. It was Callan's. A souvenir from the second world war, I believe. The police reckon it was his father's"

***

In the Horse's Head, he ordered the barbecued sausages and mashed potatoes with a pint of mild and bitter. Fiona ordered the shepherd's pie and a diet coke. When Don, the landlord, arrived with the drinks Ben said to Fiona, "I wonder where we might find this Aidan Dempsey character."

Don said, "Aidan Dempsey, the chairman of Stockport Ramblers? Had his money with that guy who died last week?"

"Yes. That's him."

Don put the two plates on the table. "He comes in here from time to time. Nice chap. Made a pile of money from electronics. Lives in Wickham Way, I believe." The landlord was always happy to help his regular customers.

"Cheers, Don," said Ben.

"Aidan Dempsey?" Fiona sipped her coke. "I thought we were looking for an Alan Dempsey."

Ben shrugged. "Maybe he has a brother."

***

They called to Aidan Dempsey's house. Mrs Dempsey answered the door. She was an elderly woman wearing two pairs of spectacles, one on her nose, the other hanging on a cord around her neck.

Ben made the introductions and asked to speak with her husband.

Mrs Dempsey shook her head. "He's not here. Could you call back?"

"How long has he been away?"

"Ten days."

"Does he have a brother?" asked Fiona.

Mrs Dempsey shook her head. "No."

Back in the car, Fiona said, "So we can forget about Mr. Dempsey."

"Looks like it," said Ben.

***

Axel Greenway was not at his office. Ben dropped Fiona off and drove around to Greenway's house. If Callan's house was opulent, Greenway's was palatial. A wide gravel driveway led up to a majestic set of steps and a massive wooden front door framed by Doric pillars.

The doorbell was answered by a tall guy dressed as a penguin who took Ben's card and steered him into the 'study'. The walls were festooned with beautifully crafted mahogany shelves festooned with beautifully crafted books, not there to be read, but entirely for effect.

When Mrs Greenway arrived she was dressed in a strapless lounge dress which spiralled across and around her body, designed to conceal any imperfections in her figure. It was doing a fine job. She held out a lank hand in a gesture straight from an old British colonial B-movie. Ben was unsure how to respond. He took hold of her wrist and kissed the back of her hand with feeling.

She retrieved her hand and flashed a sickly smile at him. "May I ask what business you have with my husband?"

"I'm investigating the death of his business partner."

She paled, took a step backwards, and left the room without another word.

Greenway entered shortly afterwards. "Mr Stone? What can I do for you?" He looked stressed and dog tired. Ben estimated his age at forty-five.

"I am here in connection with the death of your partner, Mike Callan."

Greenway said, "I can assure you, Mr Stone, that the Callan group of companies will do everything possible to protect the interests of its clients ..." He rang a small bell.

Ben tried to interrupt, "That's not why ..."

"... We have made a full statement to that effect to the press. I have nothing to add. Now if you will be so good as to leave."

The penguin reappeared with his twin and they positioned themselves behind Ben, one at each elbow.

"I am not here on behalf of the investors," said Ben.

"Whom do you represent?" asked Greenway.

"That I cannot divulge, but I am investigating the circumstances of Mr. Callan's death ..."

In response to a nod from Axel Greenway, the two penguins clamped Ben's arms in their wings and propelled him toward the front door. Ben had the sensation that his feet had sprouted wheels.

***

Early the next day, day 9, Ben found the sports holdall on his desk with a note from his daughter. It read: 'Hi Dad. Sorry I missed you again. I found your dirty tennis things and put them in the wash. Glad to see you are getting some exercise at last! Who's your mystery tennis companion? Lots of love, Lucy.'

He opened the bag and found two complete sets of white tennis clothes, one male, one female, now beautifully laundered and ironed. The female clothes bore the monogram 'Sylvia'.

Following a trip to the local patisserie, Ben place a chocolate éclair in the fridge. He had just begun to consume a second one when the phone rang.

"This is Alison Callan, Mr Stone. Could you call to the house? I don't want to speak on the phone."

"Yes, of course." Ben could feel that old tingle-of-treasure feeling again spreading from his temples to his scalp.

Within fifteen minutes his car entered the Callan property and he drove toward the house. The gardener was perched high on a ladder clipping one of the huge hedges. Ben stopped and called out to him. The man ignored him. Ben recognized the man he had seen enter the house with Mrs Callan four days earlier.

In the Callans' front living-room, Mrs. Callan sat perched on the edge of her chair. "Thank you for coming so promptly, Mr Stone."

"That's quite all right, Mrs Callan."

"Please call me Alison. May I call you Ben? First names are so much easier and much more civilized, don't you think?"

"Yes, of course, Alison. What can I do for you?"

"Well first of all, I want to be totally honest with you. Can I be sure that you will treat anything I say in the strictest confidence?"

"But of course. You can rely on my absolute discretion," said Ben, solemnly.

"Good. Well, I have a confession to make." Ben's heartrate doubled. "It's about my husband's income tax." She paused. "My husband was not always completely honest when it came to paying his income tax."

"I see ..." said Ben.

"He put a little money aside for a rainy day."

"Well, that's not unusual," said Ben. *Amongst the filthy rich*, he thought.

"Yes, well, the problem is that the money has disappeared."

"Where did you keep it?"

"MC had it in his locker at the tennis club, in a sports bag."

"MC?"

"Mike. All his friends call him MC."

"Not a very secure place to conceal a large amount of money."

"No, perhaps not, but MC always said it was the best place to hide it, because nobody would ever dream of looking there."

"Who had keys to the locker?"

"Mike had one, this one," she handed Ben a key, "and we kept a spare in the fridge."

"In the fridge?" Ben sounded incredulous.

"It's missing. Silly, I suppose, but he said that nobody would ever dream of looking there."

"How much are we talking about?"

"I'm not sure, but I think MC said half a million." She pulled a small handkerchief from her handbag and blew her nose.

"How do I know this is not investors' money?"

"Money is money," she replied. "Does it make a difference?"

"I wouldn't want to get mixed up in anything illegal."

"My husband is dead." She sniffed. "What he did is between him and his God. I am asking you to work for me."

"I charge thr... four hundred pounds a day plus expenses."

"That's fine, Ben. Would you like an advance now?"

Before he left, he asked, "Did you and your husband play tennis?"

She patted her coiffured hair. "Yes, but MC and I played very little. Axel Greenway, his business partner, persuaded him to join, but he kept his membership up for business reasons only."

"So Axel plays?"

"Yes. Both Axel and Sylvia, are very active members of the club."

"Just one more thing," said Ben. "Do you know anyone by the name of Alan Dempsey?"

She shook her head. "No, sorry. I don't think so."

Ben stopped by the bank to deposit Mrs. Callan's cheque before returning to the office. Fiona had the kettle on and a half dozen croissants hot from the patisserie.

The headline in Fiona's newspaper read:

£4M MISSING FROM CALLAN FUND.

Ben laughed. "So much for Alison's honesty."

"I beg your pardon?" said Fiona.

"Never mind. I want you to see what you can find out about the Callans' gardener. And find out who Sylvia Greenway plays tennis with."

"Right," said Fiona. She kissed him lightly on the cheek. "See you later."

When Fiona left, Ben rang the 'Busy Cockerel' and booked a table for lunch; he was flush.

There was a knock at the door. It swung open and Inspector Hackett stepped inside.

Ben offered him coffee.

"Yes, thanks. Four sugars."

He put the kettle on again. "When's the inquest, Inspector?"

"Next Tuesday. They will return an open verdict. Everyone is sure that he committed suicide."

"But you're not convinced?"

"No."

"I understood he left a suicide note."

"Yes. The note looks genuine."

"What did it say?"

"Nothing much. 'Goodbye cruel world'. That sort of thing."

"So why do you doubt that it was suicide?" Ben, handed the inspector a steaming cup of coffee.

"Well, how many suicides make a last phone call *after* shooting themselves? And who replaced the receiver?"

"Do you have any suspects?" Inspector Hackett shook his head. "What about Axel Greenway?"

"Greenway was at a police station in Liverpool at the time, paying a speeding ticket."

The two men were silent for a moment or two. Then Ben asked about Alan Dempsey.

"We found several Alan Dempseys in the general area, but none of them is remotely connected with Callan. We found an Aidan Dempsey who has money invested with Callan's fund, but he was in London at the time of the shooting."

"And the cause of death ...?"

"Bullet wound to the chest, from very close range. Ballistics have confirmed that the gun which we found in Callan's hand was the weapon used. It is ... was registered in Callan's name."

An inspirational thought flashed into Ben's mind, but before he could capture it, the thought was gone again. "Any sign of the money?"

The inspector shook his head. "No."

"Have you asked Axel Greenway?" said Ben.

"Yes. We searched his house and his office. We found nothing."

"Have you tried his tennis club locker? Both Greenway and his wife are members ..."

The inspector made a quick call to the station. Then he asked, "Why do you think Callan rang you? Do you think he dialled the wrong number?"

Ben fetched the local telephone book. He looked up Callan's office. There were several numbers listed, but none of them resembled his own.

"What about Axel Greenway's number," Inspector Hackett suggested.

Ben checked it. "No."

"Try Alan Dempsey."

Ben checked the numbers of all entries under 'Alan Dempsey' or 'A. Dempsey'. He shook his head.

"Try Dr Edward French," said the inspector.

"Who's he?"

"Callan's doctor."

Ben checked the number. He shook his head again. "Nothing like it."

***

The jugged hare at the 'Busy Cockerel' was superb. Ben treated himself to a half-bottle of last year's Beaujolais and finished off the meal with a slice of cheesecake and an Irish Coffee.

In was close to 4 o'clock when he tottered out into the street and set off for the office. The sun was shining in that shy, almost apologetic way it does in winter.

Fiona was waiting for him in the office. "Hi Ben, you look like a man who has had good news."

"Not good news, just a good lunch."

"Right." The kettle whistled. "Coffee?"

"Nothing for me." He waved a hand and lowered himself into his chair.

"The gardener's name is Kris Mashiak," she said.

"Polish, I assume."

"Yes. He lives alone and seems to have no close friends in the area, and no relatives in this country. According to his landlady he moved out of his flat recently, leaving no forwarding address."

"I know where he's living now," said Ben. "Go on."

"There's not much more to tell. He's been working in the Callans' garden for two years."

Ben sighed. "Time to put this case into some sort of order. Let's see what we have so far. Mike Callan, investment consultant, writes a suicide note and supposedly commits suicide by shooting himself in the chest. Then he makes a phone call. He says 'Alan Dempsey' and promptly snuffs it. Someone else replaces the receiver. Four million pounds have gone missing from the firm, and from the tennis club locker."

Fiona said, "Obviously, someone killed Callan, making it look like suicide, then switched the sports bags, substituting dirty tennis clobber for the cash. His business partner, Axel Greenway would be my choice."

Ben shook his head. "Greenway has a cast iron alibi, and what about the suicide note?"

"Maybe the gardener did it, for the money and the widow."

"Maybe. Did he have a phone?"

Fiona checked the phonebook. "Yes, here he is, K. Mashiak. And Bingo! This is your number, but with the last two digits transposed."

"So Callan's last action before he died was to ring ... his gardener," said Ben. "That seems improbable.

"Also, it suggests that Mashiak was not the killer," she said.

"Did you find out who Sylvia Greenway plays tennis with?"

"She plays a lot of mixed doubles." Fiona consulted her notebook. "And with practically every man in the club. Mark Peterson, John Blanding, Graham Wright ..."

"How long is this list?"

"Edward French and Michael Grant."

"*Dr* Edward French?"

"Yes. He's a local G.P."

***

Ben went home and cooked himself a large chilli con carne. He washed it down with a bottle of German Pils and finished off the meal with a bowl of vanilla ice cream.

Just after 9:00 pm, Lucy dropped in to see him.

"Hi Lucy," he said. "You've just missed a great chilli."

"That's okay, Dad. I've eaten."

They started on the dishes. Ben outlined the investigation to Lucy while they worked.

"Tell me about this gardener," she said.

"He's Polish. He's having an affair with the victim's wife."

"And what does he look like?"

"Rugged. Muscular. I only saw him from a distance."

"He was up a ladder clipping a hedge, you said?"

"Yes."

"Nobody clips hedges in the middle of the winter," she said.

At about midnight, Fiona let herself in. Ben was in bed snoring quietly. She slipped out of her clothes and slid in beside him.

***

Ben woke up with the whole case wrapped up in his mind. Fiona cooked breakfast. He kissed her like a husband on the doorstep and set off for the office. Feeling like a millionaire, he stopped off for supplies at the patisserie.

While he waited for the kettle to boil, he rang Inspector Hackett.

"Hi, Inspector," he said. "Any sign of the money?"

"Who's that? Stone? We tried all the lockers at the tennis club, but we found nothing."

"Doesn't surprise me," said Ben. "Can you call in to my office sometime during the day? I know who committed the murder."

"Murder? You can prove it was murder?"

"Yes. No question."

"Right. I'll be there in an hour." Inspector Hackett rang off.

When the inspector arrived, Ben explained. "It was something you said that started me on the right track."

"What was that?"

"You said the gun is ... was registered to Callan."

"Well it was."

"Yes, but that reminded me. His wife said something similar. She said 'All Mike's friends call him MC.' She used the present tense."

"Indicating what?"

"Indicating that Callan is still alive."

Inspector Hackett stared at Ben. "So who committed suicide?"

"Nobody. The dead person is the Callans' gardener. He was killed to convince everybody that Callan was dead. Callan took his place. Callan wrote the suicide note, his wife identified the body. Who signed the death certificate?"

"Dr French."

"Okay, so how did you work it all out?"

"The second time I saw the gardener he was up a ladder, clipping a hedge—in winter."

"Very clever." Hackett smiled.

"We can thank my daughter Lucy for that one."

"Who is Alan Dempsey? And who made the original call?"

"Mashiak made that call. What he actually said was 'Al and MC.' He was naming his murderers: Alison and MC, Mike Callan."

The inspector gave a low whistle. "So who has the money now?"

"My guess would be Dr French."

"Tell me why the gardener rang you before he died."

"He was trying to ring someone at his flat. His landlady, perhaps." Ben stuffed half a Danish into his mouth.

"And he got a wrong number," said the inspector.

SCENE OF THE CRIME

It looks familiar.
  It should. This is where it happened. That brute ...
  Are you sure?
  How could I forget that night? It was our honeymoon.
  It hasn't changed a bit.
  Wasn't it painted blue?
  No.
  I'm sure there were more windows.
  How could there have been more windows?
  Hmm. Maybe this isn't the place.
  There's one sure way to find out.
  Right. We'll stay one night and check it out.

***

I'm sure this is where I buried him.
  Dig deeper.

***

He's not here.

Maybe it is the wrong *pension*, so.

It's not the wrong place. I remember every detail of the bistro next door. Don't you?

So what do we do now?

Get back inside, get cleaned up, get back to bed and in the morning ...

Get out.

Right.

*

You enjoyed your stay?

Yes, thank you.

Oui, bien sur, monsieur le patron.

Your French is ... remarkable, *monsieur*. We might have the pleasure of your company again, *peut etre*, sometime in the future?

Perhaps. Tell me, were you here in 1973?

Oui, monsieur. My father was *le patron* in those days. I took over after *mon père* ... after he disappeared.

He disappeared! I'm sorry to hear that. Did you ever find him?

We discovered his body in the garden, *monsieur*, under a fig tree.

He was murdered, so?

He was, *madame*.

And what of the killer?

Killers, *monsieur*. There were two of them.

Were they apprehended?

Not yet, *madame*, but if you'll wait just a few moments I may have some news for you. Ah! Here's the inspector now. *Monsieur l'Inspecteur,* this is the couple I spoke to you about on the telephone …

OF UNICORNS AND DRAGONS

– 1 –

THE WHOLE AFFAIR STARTED innocently enough. I had taken to walking briskly, early mornings and late evenings, my purpose being to stimulate my metabolic system which had become strangely sluggish. It was early one misty morning in March that I returned from my pre-prandial perambulation to discover a letter lying on the floor in the entrance hall. I picked it up, and seeing that it was addressed to my good friend and colleague Herbert Soames, I took it upstairs and placed it on the breakfast table.

Within minutes, Mrs Johnson, our housekeeper had placed a plate of steaming kippers before me and I set about the meal with a will.

By the time Soames appeared it was close to ten thirty, Mrs Johnson had set out for the shops and I had polished off two helpings of bacon and kidneys and a generous portion of her excellent eggs Benedict. Soames was dressed in his favourite lounge coat which covers his ample frame from neck to ankle. He picked up the letter.

"Great Heavens, Wilson!" he exclaimed. "Have you seen this letter?"

"Yes, Soames. I discovered it in the hallway on my return this morning."

"Intriguing, don't you think?"

"Is it?" I replied, a little testily. I was taken aback by his question, given that Soames had not yet opened the missive.

He handed it to me. "Look at the envelope, Wilson."

It was of a durable paper, light grey in colour. Baffled, I shook my head.

"Observe the monogram on the reverse side," said Soames.

I turned the letter over to find the monogram 'de Farr' embossed on the flap of the envelope. I recognised it on the instant.

"It's from Piggy!" I exclaimed.

Piggy de Farr had the distinction of sharing a number of his latter school years with myself and Soames. The sobriquet, while unfortunate, was sadly apt, for de Farr had a small upturned, distinctly porcine nose and a tendency to obesity, no doubt inherited.

Soames nodded, spreading a thick layer of salted butter on a triangle of toast. "And what of the stamp?"

"There is none," I replied. "The letter must have been delivered by hand."

"Indubitably, Wilson. And when do you suppose it was delivered?"

"It must have been delivered while I was out walking."

"Very good, Wilson," said Soames through a mouthful of buttered toast.

I was astounded, for we had neither of us set eyes on the redoubtable Piggy since our school days.

There followed something of a protracted pause while Soames attended to the demands of his appetite. I knew he was not going to be able to resist the kidneys, so I opened *The Times.* Holding it up in front of me with much noisy rustlings and a few pointed coughs, I attempted to read the headlines, but try as I might I could not divert my thoughts from the mysterious letter. Human curiosity, once aroused, is a powerful force. Indeed, I have often ventured the opinion that the very evolution of civilisation as we know it may have depended to a large extent upon it. One can only wonder to what cultural and anthropological backwater mankind would have wandered if our earliest ancestors had not had the pigheadedness to discover how to tame fire, for example, or the chicken.

It was apparent that my curiosity was not going to be satisfied in the near future, as Soames continued with his breakfast, resolutely working his way through the remains of the bacon and the kidneys, masticating each morsel with infinite care. Finally, he turned his attention to the eggs Benedict, which by now must have been stuck to the platter. I caught myself grinding my teeth in exasperation.

Quite suddenly, Soames said: "Aren't you going to open it, Wilson?"

"Open what?" I replied, obtusely.

"De Farr's letter."

"It's not addressed to me, Soames."

"That's all right, Wilson. Please open it."

I put the newspaper down and opened Piggy's letter using Soames's ivory letter-opener.

As a schoolboy, Michael 'Piggy' de Farr was an unruly mess. Throughout his years at Chesterhouse, he remained sadly slovenly in every area of personal grooming. His fingers were never free of ink marks, as were his ears, his mouth, his piggy nose and even his legs; his hair looked like last year's abandoned hedgehog nest, his knees a riot of scabs in various stages of repair. Sartorially, the kindest way of describing him would have been 'unkempt'. In all the years that I knew him, I cannot recall a single occasion when his stockings were at full mast or his shirt tucked into his trousers; the knot of his tie was always somewhere behind his left ear, and his shoelaces had lives of their own. One would have been hard pressed to find a scruffier individual in all the long history of that great school.

The missive that unfolded from the envelope was Piggy on paper. It consisted of a single page liberally covered in inkblots and smudged finger marks. The handwriting was grotesque, the strokes of the pen at times bold and sweeping, but more often weak, hesitant, barely leaving a mark. The writing was recognisably Piggy's.

I cleared my throat and read aloud:

"Dear Sherbet. . ."

I grinned at Soames. The long forgotten nickname threatened to release a flood of boyhood memories. Soames waved his fork at me impatiently. "Read on," he commanded.

"Dear Sherbet,

"Forgive my presumption in writing to you after so many years, but I am in dire something–– of your help. I am in dire need of your help. My father is dead and I am to be–– I can't make out the next word–– in his place. There have already been two attempts on my life. I can trust nobody here. Please come at once. It is signed: Your friend Michael de Farr."

I looked up from the letter to see Soames beaming across the table at me, a stringy piece of spinach lodged between his front teeth.

"The words 'presumption' and 'dire' are misspelt," I added.

"Good old Piggy," said Soames.

"Poor spelling is hardly a matter for adulation," I protested.

"Never mind the spelling, Wilson. What about the content of the letter?"

"It sounds like gibberish to me, Soames."

"I think not, Wilson. Remember how de Farr hated writing."

"About as much as he hated bathing," I said grimly.

"He would do anything to avoid picking up a pen."

I nodded.

"Well there you are, then. The very fact that he took the trouble to write to us suggests that his concern for his personal safety is genuine, wouldn't you say?"

"You mean Piggy's life really is in danger?"

"Undoubtedly, Wilson."

– 2 –

There is something very relaxing about a train journey. The rhythmical clickety-clack of wheels on track, the occasional high pitched, animal-like wail of urgency from the whistle, and the violent swaying from side to side all add to the wonderful feeling of reckless speed. But for me, the most abiding memory of train journeys is the smell of soot wafting in through the open windows. Even now, the smallest whiff of soot from a coal fire will bring locomotives instantly to my mind and tears to my eyes.

We had a compartment to ourselves, and we sat facing each other by the window. It was a no smoking compartment-- there were signs to that effect over every seat-- but Soames lit his pipe, and I raised no objection.

Sitting opposite Soames, watching him tinkering with his pipe, I could not but marvel at the dexterity with which he handled this enormous fiery instrument. It seemed to me that his nasal hairs, bountiful as they were, were constantly at risk of immolation, and yet they never caught fire, nor were they ever singed, to the best of my knowledge.

I sighed contentedly. This trip to the Dorset countryside promised to be a good old fashioned tonic to both of us. Soames and I have been friends for many years, and it would be hard to imagine a finer fellowship. However, it had been some weeks since our last case and through constant exposure to his company over an extended period in the confines of our apartments, I must confess that I was starting to find his eccentric personality just a little tiresome.

Soames pointed the stem of his pipe at me. "What do we know of de Farr's family, Wilson?"

I searched my mind for old discarded memories of long forgotten conversations with Piggy. The effort brought a frown to my face. I replied: "His father was a duke, I believe."

"The duke of Bishop-Salford."

"So if the duke is dead –"

Soames nodded. "Piggy is the new duke of Bishop-Salford."

At that precise moment, the train lurched violently, flinging open the door to the corridor, and a man fell full length into the compartment and onto the floor at our feet. He was tall, perhaps fifty-five years old, thin to the point of emaciation. His dress suggested a labourer or an indentured servant of some kind.

Together, Soames and I helped him to his feet. Instantly, I found myself staring into two small piercing eyes astride a nose like a hatchet; the man's skin was cratered with pock-marks. The expression on his face was one of undisguised hatred, of violence barely restrained. He drew his palm across his face, revealing the tattoo of a unicorn on the back of his hand, before mumbling something incoherent and disappearing back into the corridor.

"I wondered when he was going to introduce himself," said Soames to the bowl of his pipe.

"I beg your pardon, Soames?"

"Our friend the postman."

"The postman?"

"Yes. Surely you noticed him earlier. He followed us from Barber Street to Waterloo station and on to the train."

I stared at Soames in disbelief, for in truth I had not observed the man before.

Soames chuckled. "I think we may assume that he is the one who delivered de Farr's letter. Probably one of the duke's footmen."

"Or a gardener, perhaps," I said, recovering some of my composure.

"Definitely a footman," said Soames. He waited for me to ask how he had worked this out, but I said nothing. Undeterred, he resumed: "You will have noticed the fraying of his cuffs and the way his shoes were scuffed at the toes and the outer edges?"

I shook my head.

"Also, the knees of his britches were worn almost threadbare."

"So why has he been following us?" I interjected.

Soames shrugged. "He is probably acting under instructions."

"Piggy's instructions?" I ventured.

Soames raised his eyebrows in affirmation.

"And what of his facial disfigurement, Wilson?"

"Undoubtedly the result of an earlier encounter with smallpox or the syphilis. Either way, the unfortunate fellow will carry the scars with him for the rest of his life."

Soames was peering down into the bowl of his pipe like a man in search of lost treasure. "Unfortunate he may be, Wilson," he said. "But there are many less fortunate than he."

"In the cemetery, you mean?"

"Precisely so," said Soames.

***

We arrived at Bishop-Salford station as dusk was falling. As we alighted from the train, our pock-marked friend was close by. He stood poorly concealed behind a pillar watching as I loaded our luggage on board an open carriage.

I instructed the driver to take us to Charlington Manor. At the mention of our destination, the driver blanched visibly.

"The maanor?"

"Charlington Manor," I confirmed.

"But it be gatherin' daark," the driver objected.

"Yes, so let's get a move on, man," I said.

"You'd best not go there after daark, sir."

"Whyever not, man?" I snapped at him.

"There be things ..."

"Things?"

"Things that 'aappen there at noight. 'Awrrible things ..."

"What sort of things?"

Soames had been engrossed in my newspaper. "Is there a problem?" He enquired.

"Nothing I cannot handle," I replied.

"Will you take us to the manor?" I asked the driver. "Or should we engage another carriage?"

"Oi'll take you there, young sir, but don't you say as you 'aaven't 'ad fair waarnin'." With that, he cracked his whip fiercely across the horse's back and the carriage shot forward with such force that I was thrown back into my seat.

– 3 –

We approached the great house from a height, rounding a bend in the road to see it nestling in a valley and surrounded on three sides by extensive lawns, terraces, and mature oak woodland. An involuntary gasp escaped my lips. The great mansion was breathtaking in both size and scale, perfectly symmetrical in every detail and with impressive turrets on every corner.

We dismounted. I unloaded the luggage and the carriage sped off at a gallop back down the long driveway and into the gathering gloom.

We were received at the door and escorted to one of the drawing rooms by an old butler in full morning dress and white gloves. From within, the manor seemed even larger than it appeared from without, an impression perhaps accentuated by the fact that it was bathed in an unnatural gloom, being but sparsely lit.

The silence of the place was spine-chilling. Soames and I have visited many country estates during the course of our investigations, and we were accustomed to the bustling sounds of a large country house. Apart from ticking and chiming of clocks and the creaking and groaning of the timbers, there should have been distant sounds of dripping water, curtains rustling, windows rattling, doors opening and closing, and a multitude of other sounds – small animals scampering through the wainscoting, bats in the attic, death-watch beetles munching their way through wood panelling. This great house was silent as the grave.

The drawing room was dominated by a large fireplace of black marble, topped by a large mirror in a gilt frame. No fire filled the hearth, but even so, it provided a magnificent centrepiece to the room. Soames strolled over and proceeded to inspect each and every ornament displayed on the mantle.

I had just unbuttoned my coat and was lowering myself wearily into a large chaise longue when Piggy rushed into the room, hurried over to Soames and shook him warmly by the hand.

"Soames, my old friend, thank you for coming."

Soames recovered his hand and said: "De Farr, this is Wilson. You remember Wilson. He was at school with us."

Piggy looked at me. "Sniffy Wilson," he said. "Yes of course I remember. Welcome, old boy." He shook my hand vigorously.

"Hello, Piggy," I said, trading sobriquets. Soames glared at me over Piggy's shoulder, but Piggy seemed unaffected – perhaps even pleased – by the appellation. He gestured for us to sit and began to relate his story.

"I am under siege," he began, "by a ruthless and persistent criminal assassin."

"My God, Piggy!" I exclaimed.

Soames flashed a recriminatory glance in my direction and said, "Tell us what has transpired, de Farr. Take your time and spare us no detail."

"It started with the beet," said de Farr.

"The beet," Soames echoed.

"Yes. You see we have an excellent kitchen garden on the estate and each year we are blessed with copious quantities of light vegetables, lettuce, leeks, celery, tomatoes, cucumber –"

"And beet." Soames suggested.

"And beet. Yes. Beet is one of my particular favourites. When beet is in season, I eat a lot of it. I'd have beet in vinegar at luncheon, beet soup at dinner. Sometimes I would take small amounts of beet with my porridge for breakfast in the morning."

"You are fond of the stuff, then?" I suggested.

Piggy continued: "About a week after my father died, I discovered that my beet was poisoned."

Soames's eyebrows twitched visibly.

"As luck would have it, I gave some to Truffles, one of our old dogs, and he dropped dead at my feet."

"Great Heavens, Piggy!" I cried.

"So you didn't eat any of the poisoned vegetable yourself?" Soames said.

"Not a morsel. I am certain that I would not be talking to you now if I had but tasted the deadly stuff."

"And the poison? You discovered what it was?" I asked, my scientific curiosity aroused.

"The police had it analysed. It was a powerful toxin, derived from the venom of a reptile."

"How extraordinary!" I exclaimed.

"This reptile, what species was it, do you know?" Soames asked, fishing his pipe from his breast pocket.

"A Komodo dragon," Piggy replied.

"How astonishing!" I exclaimed.

Soames nodded. "The venom of the Komodo dragon is a foul smelling fast acting toxicant," he said, peering into the bowl of his pipe. "Quite lethal, but not commonly used as a poison."

"I expect it is difficult to come by," I suggested.

"In England, certainly," Soames replied. "But it is almost worthless to the poisoner as the odour is so difficult to disguise."

"And beet –"

"– would have been the ideal disguise," said Soames. "And what of your father?" he asked Piggy. "Was he murdered?"

Piggy's eyes widened in shock. He shook his head. "He died six weeks ago, of heart failure. We buried him in the local cemetery, in the family vault."

"My condolences," said Soames solemnly.

"Yes, and mine, old man," I added.

"Thank you both. His passing was a great loss to the family."

"Was he elderly?" I enquired.

"Eighty-seven."

"He was in poor health?" asked Soames, shovelling tobacco into his pipe.

"Fit as a fiddle."

"And the cause of death was heart failure, you say?"

"Yes. His death was certified by the family doctor."

"And there was no inquest," Soames mused thoughtfully.

"No. The police were satisfied that there was no doubt about the cause of death."

"And you are satisfied that he died of natural causes?" I asked.

"He was old. He died. What could be more natural than that?"

"And you had no cause to suspect foul play?" I persisted.

He looked up at me sharply. Before he could reply, the door burst open and a large woman entered. Instantly recognisable as Piggy's sister, she bore all of the family features: the tendency to obesity, the upturned snub nose with wide pronounced nostrils. She had Piggy's flushed complexion and his small eyes, set just a fraction too close together.

By means of a rapid series of jerky hip movements, and with surprising speed, she advanced across the room towards Soames, flinging out a podgy arm in greeting.

"Herbert Soames," she cried, shaking his hand in both of hers. "I am delighted to make your acquaintance. I am Rebecca de Farr."

"Enchanted," said Soames. "My condolences on the loss of your father."

She dropped Soames's hand and turned to face me. "And this is …?"

"Wilson," I said. "Doctor Reginald Wilson. Soames and I work closely together."

She shook my hand and lowered her frame carefully onto a settee.

"I take it there were other incidents, de Farr?" said Soames as he lit his pipe.

"There was the death of the undergardener," replied Piggy

"Betteridge," Rebecca snorted.

Piggy continued: "He was found in the conservatory."

"Found? Great heavens, Piggy, you don't mean he was killed?"

Piggy nodded. "Yes, but I believe that I was the intended target."

Soames said, "Please explain."

"I usually have my afternoon tea in the conservatory. On this particular occasion, I had taken a detour to the study to fetch a new book. I had just finished one, you see – Bleak House, by Charles Dickens. Have you read Dickens, by the by – either of you?"

"And while you were in the study fetching a book … ?" Soames prompted, blowing great clouds of smoke from his pipe.

"I was away for no more than a few minutes, and when I returned I found poor Betteridge. He was sitting in my chair. The housekeeper was attempting to revive him, but he was beyond help."

"Dead?" I gasped.

"As a gatepost."

"And how was he killed?" Asked Soames.

Piggy and Rebecca exchanged a glance.

"He carried the mark," said Piggy.

"And what was this mark?" I asked.

Rebecca's nostrils flared. "The mark of the horned beast," she hissed.

— 4 —

Soames removed his pipe and opened his mouth, but said nothing.

Piggy explained. "A small circular incision at the back of the neck. The locals have identified it as the mark of the unicorn."

At this, Soames and I exchanged a glance. During the course of our investigations, there are times when we are confronted by ignorance and superstition. As practicing scientists, we would never give credence to such nonsense, of course, but we both recognise the powerful nature of these ancient beliefs, many of which have been passed down through the generations for hundreds, or even thousands, of years.

Soames said: "Betteridge was stabbed in the neck, you say?"

Piggy and Rebecca nodded in unison.

"And the wound was circular?" I asked.

"Circular, yes," agreed his lordship. "About one sixteenth of an inch in diameter."

"The mark of the unicorn!" Rebecca cried. "No question about it."

***

Before dinner we met Mrs Parks, the housekeeper. She was a diminutive lady of perhaps sixty years with a mottled red complexion, her grey hair tied in a severe bun at the back.

Piggy introduced us. "Mrs Parks and her husband, Henry, have been with the family for – How long has it been, Mrs Parks?"

"Close on twenty years, my lord."

After she had left the scene, Piggy explained: "Henry Parks is the head gardener. Mrs Parks is our cook as well as our housekeeper. It is difficult to keep servants in this neck of the woods."

Dinner was a sombre affair. The meal was served by Fortesque, the butler, assisted by a short, plump scullery maid called Gladys Abbott. Fortesque was an entirely unremarkable man of average height and stocky build, in his late sixties. Like all of the best butlers, he was the sort of man who could easily pass for a piece of the furniture.

Gladys was an entirely different matter. She was fully forty years old with what the euphemists would describe as an ample figure, and with blonde hair in ringlets which would have been much more at home on an infant. She was impossible to ignore, dressed as she was in a black and white costume several sizes too small. She had a tendency to clumsiness, making it advisable to watch her every move as she manoeuvred our dishes in front of us.

The first course was an attempt at consommé, but it was far too salty and served lukewarm, which spoiled it for me. Soames did not seem to notice.

As Gladys was clearing away the soup bowls, Soames said to the young duke: "I think we may have met one of your servants in London."

"That would be Catchpole, the footman," Piggy replied. "It was he who delivered my letter to you. Catchpole is a reformed convict. Upon his release from prison, my father took him in and given him employment, and he has served the family faithfully ever since."

"He was released from prison, you say?" I could not disguise my amazement.

Piggy nodded.

"Of what crime was he convicted?"

"Murder."

"Great heavens, Piggy!"

"He served twelve years in Broadmore. While in prison he discovered religion and when he came out he was a changed man. There's not a violent bone left in his body."

"Tell them about the lizards," Rebecca said sharply.

Piggy nodded. "Catchpole keeps – kept – a large collection of lizards."

"Including a Komodo dragon," said Soames thoughtfully. It should have been a question, but Soames felt no need of the question mark.

Piggy nodded.

"Whom did he kill?" I asked.

"Don't you recall the case, Wilson?" Soames said. "It was about twenty years ago. He slew his landlady, Mary Monk. He slit her throat and made off with her jewels."

Once again, I had cause to marvel at my colleague's incredible powers of recall. When it comes to criminals and crimes, Soames has the memory of a herd of elephants.

"And he escaped the gallows – how?" I queried.

"As I recall, the victim's husband was tried for the murder and found guilty. Catchpole confessed to the crime some years later."

"And he escaped the hangman because ...?"

"I assume the judge was influenced by the fact that an innocent man had already been hanged for the crime."

"All the more reason to send the true murderer to the gallows, I would have thought."

"Even so, Catchpole was sentenced to life imprisonment."

"And the landlady's husband was convicted of the crime, you say."

Piggy nodded vigorously. "Albert Monk. He was a well-known member of the London criminal underclass. No-one was surprised when he was convicted."

"And he was executed." I swallowed hard. The vicissitudes occasioned by Lady Justice are sometimes hard to stomach; her infamous blindfold is as much a curse as a benison.

"Yes," replied Piggy. "He went to the gallows protesting his innocence."

"Tell me, de Farr," Soames interjected, "did Catchpole contract the smallpox at some point?"

"Yes, while serving his prison sentence. He still carries the scars."

"And he has lost his violent tendencies?" Soames enquired.

"Completely," said Piggy. "He was paroled about five years ago after serving a mere twelve years of his life sentence."

"Curiouser and curiouser," I said.

"Not really," Piggy explained. "I believe someone of influence spoke up for him."

"Your father the duke?" Soames suggested.

"Precisely so," Piggy replied.

***

Shortly after the meal Soames and I were shown to our rooms. At the head of the stairs there hung a huge portrait of the seventh duke – Randolph – dressed in colourful doublet and hose, an enormous menacing stag peering over his left shoulder. He was sporting an impressive sword in a scabbard and I immediately spotted the now familiar unicorn tattoo on the back of his hand as it rested on the butt of the sword. I pointed this out to Soames.

Directly upon entering my room, I prepared for bed. The hour was not late, but it had been a long, gruelling day, and I was uncommonly tired. I tossed my clothes onto the back of a chair without bothering to fold them, climbed into the bed, blew out the candle and fell asleep right away.

***

I awoke with a start. It was pitch dark. I could see nothing, but I sensed there was someone – or *something* in the room. I lay very still and strained to hear the intruder's breathing, but I could hear only my own. I considered lighting the candle, but I was unsure where the matches were.

My pistol was out of reach in the pocket of my greatcoat which I had thrown across my suitcase.

I became convinced that there was a small animal in the room with me. A scuttling scratching sound near the door, then by the end of the bed confirmed my worst fears: whatever it was, was moving around the room. From the scuttling sounds, I tried to calculate the size of the beast, but I could not. To my ears the sound suggested a dragon of the size slain by St. George. Then I was assailed by an even more alarming thought: perhaps there was more than one of them.

I am not a timid person and have had occasional encounters with all manner of beasts – indeed, I kept a wild tortoise for several years as a child – but I own that my heart was beating fiercely by the time I managed to locate the matches and light the candle by my bed.

A thorough search of the room revealed nothing. It was close to four a.m. and as I had no knowledge which rooms Soames or Piggy occupied, I blew out the candle and tried to go back to sleep.

– 5 –

I arose early, dressed, and made my way down to breakfast. To my surprise, Soames was there ahead of me, a full plate of greasy black and white pudding on the table before him.

"Good morning, Wilson. Sleep well?"

"Not really, Soames, thanks to an intruder."

Soames raised an eyebrow.

"I woke up at about four a.m. to find someone or *something* in my room."

"Who or what was it?"

"I cannot say," I replied. "It was dark. It might have been lizards."

"More than one?"

"Possibly. I cannot say for certain."

"But you did confront him – it – them?"

"No, Soames. I thought it more prudent not to."

"So what transpired?"

"It – whatever it was – scuttled about the room for a bit and then disappeared."

Soames gave me one of his withering looks – one of those looks usually reserved for Mrs Johnson when his warming pan is not at the required temperature or his shirts are not starched to perfection.

"There really was nothing I could do," I protested. "By the time I managed to light my candle, I was alone again in the room."

"You did the right thing so, Wilson," Soames said in a tone which suggested otherwise.

I began to help myself to some breakfast. The adventure of the night had given me a healthy appetite.

Soames said: "After breakfast, you might accompany me on a tour of the grounds, Wilson. There are a number of matters which we need to discuss."

The scream hit us before I could respond. Such a blood-curdling scream I have seldom heard. It came from close by and echoed from the walls around us like the tolling of a great bell. Soames was up and running. I dropped my cutlery on the plate and followed him.

Piggy's body lay on the carpet in the vestibule. Catch-pole the footman was close by. Mrs Parks stood by the doorway, her hand stuffed in her mouth to stifle her screams.

Piggy was fully dressed. He was lying on his right side near an open door, his eyes staring straight ahead, as if he were attempting to follow the progress of some insect crawling across the carpet. I checked for signs of life and found none. Piggy's body was still warm, but the spark of his life had departed beyond the reach of medical science.

Soames bent down to examine Piggy's head. There was a small circular wound at the base of his skull at the back, and very little blood.

"This is not a bullet wound," I said. "It's a stab wound, but obviously made with something other than a knife."

At this grisly sight, Mrs Parks gave another ear-piercing scream and ran off.

***

The head gardener was despatched to the village to fetch the police and Soames and I returned to the dining room to resume our breakfast. Not that we lacked respect for the unfortunate Piggy, but our ministrations, no matter how well intentioned, could do nothing to help him, and in the meantime our food was growing cold.

"These unicorns are a puzzle," I said, hoping for some enlightenment from my learned friend.

"In what respect, Wilson?" Soames asked.

"Well for a start, why would Catchpole and the seventh Duke Randolph both carry the same strange tattoo? Do we put this down to coincidence?"

Soames shook his head. "You will have heard of the AEIOU."

"No. I don't believe I have."

"The Ancient Eclectic International Order of the Unicorn. An order founded around the time of the crusades, dedicated to the furtherance of male ambitions and aspirations."

"Maintenance of the superior social standing of men in society?"

"That sort of thing, yes." Soames nodded.

"A secret society – like the Freemasons?"

"Secret? Possibly. Secretive, certainly."

"And the tattoo is a mark of membership of this secret society?"

Soames nodded. "The unicorn is the universal symbol of the male persona, and has been used for that purpose since time immemorial."

"I don't think I follow you, Soames," I said.

"It is really quite simple, Wilson. When we contemplate the unicorn's unusual horn, what part of the male anatomy immediately springs to mind?"

"Oh, I see," I blushed. I am as broadminded as the next man, but the conversation was taking us into uncomfortable territory. "We must assume, then, that Catchpole is implicated in Piggy's murder?"

"Obviously," Soames replied. "And not just Piggy's murder, but Betteridge the undergardener's as well."

I considered this proposition for a moment.

"So both cases are solved," I said.

"Perhaps, perhaps not," Soames replied.

"But I thought that was what you said a moment ago."

"Not at all, Wilson. I merely agreed with you that *we must assume* that the footman is implicated."

"Meaning?"

"Meaning that the proposition is a reasonable working hypothesis, but we do not yet have definitive proof one way or the other."

I said, "I see," although I was now thoroughly confused.

"We must find the motive," said Soames. "To be sure, Catchpole was an ex-convict –"

" – a convicted murderer," I interjected.

"As you say, a convicted murderer, but one who had been taken in by the duke, given shelter and employment. Would he not have been grateful to his employer? Would he really have jeopardised everything that he had gained at the hands of the duke by killing one of his benefactor's servants and then his only son?"

"If it comes to that," I said. "What was the duke's motivation in helping Catchpole in the first place? Are we to believe that this was a magnificent act of heroic altruism?"

"Good question, Wilson," said Soames. "And if so, how did he come to select Catchpole as the object of this altruism? Was he selected at random? Or was there some prior connection between Catchpole and the duke?"

"Are not these questions which we must address?" I asked.

"Yes, indeed, Wilson. We must interview the footman as soon as may be."

– 6 –

Catchpole was a sullen cur. He cowered just inside the door, wringing his hands and, for the most part, staring at the floor in front of him. Had he been a dog, he would surely have had his tail tucked firmly between his hind legs. He had in his possession a sack of rough brown material, tied at the top.

"You first made the acquaintance of his lordship in India, I believe," was Soames's opening gambit.

"I did, your honour. My mother served 'is lordship in the colony."

"And you joined his employ – when?"

"Shortly after I was released from prison – about five year ago."

Inside the sack something stirred.

"Tell us about the lizards," I prompted.

"Yes, tell us about your lizards," Soames agreed.

"I've always kept them – reptiles, I mean. Ever since I was a lad."

"You had no fear of them?" I asked.

He shook his head. "No, your honour, no fear. I find them quite affectionate, in a reptilian sort of way."

"Explain," Soames insisted.

"Well, your honour, reptiles crave just two things: food and warmth. Give 'em enough food and keep 'em warm and they are 'armless creatures. They will 'appily sleep all day."

"And at night?" I asked sharply.

"Many of them are nocturnal, it's true, your honours, but even so, they are only active at night if they are 'ungry."

"You keep these lizards where?" Soames pressed.

"I keep them in a 'erpetarium in my room –"

"A herpetarium? That's an aquarium for snakes?" I said.

"Exactly, your honour, a number of large glass cases."

"How many lizards are we talking about?" Soames asked.

"I had twenty-six, your honour, but six are still at large."

"At large?"

"Yes, your honours. All twenty-six escaped –"

"When was this?" Soames demanded.

"A day or two before the dog was poisoned."

"And how did they escape?" I asked.

Catchpole shrugged. "Someone must have let them out."

"Someone entered your room and let your lizards loose. Is that what you are saying?" Soames asked.

Catchpole nodded. "Yes, your honour."

"And you have no idea who let them out?" I asked.

"No, your honour."

"So you have been rounding them up and six are still at large?"

"Yes, your honours. I have a couple of the smaller ones here is this bag."

"And the Komodo dragon?" I asked.

"Still at large."

"And are any of the others venomous breeds?" I was aghast.

"Two are gila monsters, one a small Mexican bearded dragon, your honour. The others are 'armless to 'umans."

"And are these under lock and key?"

The footman shook his head. "Still at large, your hon-ours."

I shuddered.

"Before you go," said Soames, "tell us about the tattoo on your hand,"

"The sign of the dominant sex," he replied, lifting his head and leering at us.

"That will be all for now." Soames said bringing the interview to an end.

***

After the interview, Soames and I took a stroll in the grounds. The great house was surrounded on all sides by acres of parkland set in lawn, punctuated with ornamental evergreen trees and bounded by tall hedges.

"This way," said Soames, and we set out to circumambulate the house.

"I must say, Soames," I said, "I am surprised that you have made no attempt to locate the murder weapon."

He pulled something from the pocket of his greatcoat and handed it to me. It was a small statuette of a unicorn made of ivory, exquisitely carved, and mounted on a solid marble base. The horn was about three inches long, tapering from a sharp point at the tip to about one sixteenth of an inch at the base. I was astonished.

"Where did you find this?" I gasped.

"It was on the mantle in the drawing room. I noticed it yesterday when we arrived."

"And you picked it up today – after Piggy's murder?"
He nodded.

"Where did you find it?"

"It was in its usual place on the mantle in the drawing room."

"This is almost certainly the murder weapon, Soames," I expostulated.

"Indubitably."

"The mark of the unicorn," I gasped.

"So it would seem," Soames replied.

"And the murderer?" I asked, for I would not have been surprised at that point if Soames had had a full explanation for everything that had transpired at Charlington Manor.

Soames stopped abruptly. He said: "Listen, Wilson. What do you hear?"

I did as he requested. Then I shook my head. "I hear nothing."

"And I," he replied. "Is not that remarkable?"

"How is that remarkable?"

"Surely, there should be some sounds of the countryside to regale our ears."

Soames was right, as always. In fact, the silence, once he had pointed it out to me, was quite unnerving. There was not a sound to be heard; not the lowing of cattle nor the bleating of sheep and not a tweet or twitter from any bird.

We rounded a corner of the manor and came across a dead crow lying on the grass. I bent to examine it and Soames cried out sharply: "Leave it, man."

"What danger do you suppose there could be from a dead bird?" I enquired.

"Who knows?" He replied. "Better safe than sorry, Wilson."

– 7 –

It took us the best part of thirty minutes to complete our circuit of the manor garden, by which time there was an open police carriage parked at the front door with two large black mares sweating either side of the shaft. A white covered ambulance carriage was drawing away from the house.

We repaired to the drawing room where Rebecca de Farr introduced us to Inspector Morgan and Constable Longneck of the Bishop-Salford constabulary.

"You are the detective Herbert Soames of London?" The inspector asked.

"I have that honour," Soames replied graciously.

"Your fame precedes you," the inspector said.

"You are too kind," said Soames, "although I believe my fame is perhaps a little overblown in some quarters."

"We are but simple country folk hereabouts," the inspector continued, "and as you and your companion have been present during the night, I would be most interested to hear what you make of the matter, Mr Soames."

"My companion's name is Wilson – Doctor Wilson. And we would be delighted to assist you with your investigation in any way that we can."

Morgan tipped his forelock to me and turned his attention back to Soames.

Soames placed his finger tips together and held them to his lips as if in deep thought. Then he continued thus:

"We arrived yesterday in response to a desperate request from his lordship –"

"Desperate?" Morgan interrupted.

"Oh yes," continued Soames. "We were summoned by letter as his lordship was in fear for his life."

"You have this letter?"

Soames fished the letter from an inside pocket and handed it to the inspector, who read it and handed it to his constable.

"You were previously acquainted with his lordship?"

"We were at school together – all three of us."

"Please continue, Mr Soames."

"Unfortunately our presence was not sufficient to prevent the tragic death of our dear friend. We have, however, determined the following facts which may expedite your investigation. Firstly, the young duke was killed in exactly the same way as was his undergardener, Betteridge – by a single stabbing blow to the back of the neck. I managed to secure the murder weapon and I now offer it to you for safe-keeping." At this, Soames produced the ivory unicorn and handed it to the inspector. "Second, his lordship informed us before his tragic death that an earlier attempt had been made on his life by a beet laced with a deadly poison. This attempt failed only because the offending vegetable was consumed – in part – by one of his lordship's dogs."

"The poison was identified as venom from a large lizard." This time the interruption was from Constable Longneck.

"Indeed, Constable," Soames resumed. "A Komodo dragon, one of the reptiles which the footman, Catchpole, had in his herpetarium and which – he says – escaped or were released mysteriously." He turned back to the inspector. "May I ask, Inspector, whether you were in charge of the investigations of the poisoning of the dog and the murder of Betteridge, the undergardener?"

"I was. I am." Morgan replied.

"And may I ask whether you have reached any conclusions on these matters?"

"Not as yet, Mr Soames. The footman is our main suspect for both crimes, but we have insufficient evidence to charge him with either."

"And your reasons for suspecting him?"

"For the poisoning, I believe he would be the only person capable of lacing a beet with the toxin from a Komodo dragon – a beast which he kept in his room."

"And for the murder?"

"In the first place he bears the tattoo mark of the unicorn – no doubt you have observed this?" Soames nodded. "And second, we have it on good authority that he had a violent argument with the undergardener shortly before he was killed."

"And your authority for this violent argument?"

"Henry Parks, the head gardener."

– 8 –

Upon the suggestion of the butler, Fortesque, we all repaired to the study where the inspector positioned himself behind a large desk. Rebecca de Farr was interviewed first. She sat bolt upright on a straight-backed chair and answered all of the questions put to her without a moment's hesitation.

"Miss de Farr," the inspector began. "With regard to the murder of the undergardener, Betteridge, where were you at that time?"

"I was in this room, inspector, reading, when my brother came looking for a book to read."

"And which book did he select?" Asked Soames.

"Nicholas Nickleby, by Charles Dickens."

"And when your brother was killed, you were where?"

"I was in the oratory tending to my morning devotions."

Soames raised an eyebrow. "This is a regular habit of yours, Miss de Farr?"

"Yes."

The inspector continued: "May I ask you, Miss de Farr, do you have any idea who might have killed the undergardener or your brother?"

"I believe that Parks, the head gardener may have had a hand in Betteridge's killing."

"And your reasoning?" Asked Soames.

"My brother intended to let Parks go and promote Betteridge to the position of head gardener. Parks would never have allowed that to happen."

"I see," said the inspector, thoughtfully. "And do you consider that sufficient motive for Parks to have killed his lordship the duke as well?"

"Yes. Of course the footman, Catchpole is an equally likely suspect for both murders as I am sure you must realise."

"How so?"

"My brother hated the footman, and Catchpole knew that sooner or later, Michael would find an excuse to discharge him, once our father was dead."

"Your father favoured Catchpole?"

"Yes. They had a special bond, which my brother did not share."

"The AEIOU?" Soames surmised.

"Just so," Rebecca confirmed.

"And why would Catchpole wish to kill the undergardener?"

"I thought it was obvious that Betteridge may have been killed in mistake for my brother."

"They were sufficiently alike to be mistaken for each other?" The question was mine.

"Yes, Dr Wilson, in stature, colouring and in build."

"And are there others in the household whom we should consider suspect?" the inspector pressed.

"Fortesque, our butler," she replied. "My brother told him after the death of our father that he intended to replace him. I believe he might have killed Michael for that reason."

"And Betteridge?"

She shrugged. "In mistake for Michael."

Mrs Parks, the housekeeper, was the next to be interviewed. Before the inspector could frame his first question, she produced a pair of dirty white gloves from the folds of her gown an handed them to Constable Longneck. The constable passed them to the inspector, who gave them to Soames.

"My husband found these in amongst the compost," she said.

"When did he find them?" The inspector asked.

"A few days after the lizards escaped." She shuddered. "Shortly after the dog was poisoned."

"And you or he did not think to present them to us before now?" the inspector asked pointedly.

"I was not sure that they had any bearing on your investigation."

"And now you think that they may have?"

"Yes."

I observed that Soames was holding the gloves close to his nose. He said: "These gloves must have been used to administer the poisoned beet that killed the dog. I can smell the toxin. The smell is faint, but still distinguishable and see here where the red of the beet has left a stain."

The inspector began his questioning by asking the housekeeper if she could provide an alibi for her husband for each of the murders.

"Yes, of course, he was with me on both occasions."

"And yet he was absent on both occasions when you discovered the bodies – that of the undergardener and the body of your master." Soames's tone was tart.

The inspector held up his hand before Mrs Parks could answer. "We do not seriously suspect your husband Mrs Parks. It seems that these foul deeds may be laid at the door of others."

"Indeed, yes, sir," she responded. "I believe you should look closely at her ladyship for the murder of the undergardener."

I was amazed at this. I blurted out: "Lady Rebecca? What possible motive could she have to slay the undergardener?"

"A lover's tiff, perhaps?" She replied slyly.

"They were lovers?" Soames was astonished at this revelation.

"Indeed, sir. As are Gladys Abbott and the footman, Catchpole."

I took a moment to reflect. This woman was a font of information!

"You found his lordship's body?" Soames asked.

"Yes, sir."

"Tell us what happened."

"I left the kitchen to find Gladys. I found his lordship lying in the vestibule."

"And what time was this?"

"Nine-thirty or thereabouts."

"And was he dead when you found him?"

"I really can't say, sir. He looked unwell."

"Unwell? Was he breathing?"

"I don't think so, sir."

Gladys the maid, was the next to be interviewed. The inspector began by asking: "Where were you when the body of the young duke was discovered?"

"I was in my room, sir."

"I must warn you," the inspector said, "that we have been informed that you and the footman, Catchpole, have been having an affair."

She blushed visibly. Her eyes darted about the room. She opened her mouth to speak but no sound emerged.

"I ask you again," said the inspector gravely, "where were you when Mrs Parks discovered the body?"

"I was in Mr Catchpole's room, sir."

"You spent the night there?"

"Yes, sir."

"And what of Catchpole? Did he leave the room at any time during the night?"

In response to the inspector's question, the maid's eyes again darted about the room. Soames glanced at Inspector Morgan, the inspector gave an almost imperceptible nod and Soames dismissed the maid.

The head gardener was the next to be interviewed. He was a small man with a dark, swarthy complexion and big hands. His fingernails were encrusted with dirt and he seemed to be chewing something as he spoke.

"You are Henry Parks, the head gardener?"

"Your humble servant, sir."

"The husband of Mrs Parks," Soames said.

"For my sins, sir, for my sins."

The attempt at humour was ignored by all present.

"And where were you when his lordship's body was discovered?"

"I were in the garden, sir." The tone of voice and the expression on the man's face were of patient indulgence, as if the question could only have been posed by a child or a complete half-wit.

"And when your wife discovered Betteridge's body?" Soames gave no reaction to the man's impudence.

"I were in the garden, sir, as I told the inspector before."

"We have been told that the young duke intended to dismiss you."

"I know nothing of that, sir."

"Apparently, Betteridge was to take your place as head gardener."

"Over my dead body, sirs."

"Perhaps you killed Betteridge to frustrate the young duke's plan?" I suggested.

"No, sir. That is not true. I am not a killing sort of person. Ask anyone you wish."

***

Later that afternoon, after a passable luncheon of small game, Soames informed Inspector Morgan that he had solved the case.

"There are just a few minor details to resolve, for which I will require the participation of the entire household – in the drawing room," he said.

Rebecca de Farr sat in splendid isolation on her favourite settee. Parks and his wife sat close together by one of the windows. Catchpole sat on the head gardener's other side. Dressed as usual in full morning suit and white gloves, Fortesque declined to sit; he stood bolt upright close to Constable Longneck by the door. Soames and Inspector Morgan stood on either side of the marble fireplace. I occupied the chaise longue.

"Thank you all for coming," Soames began. "I believe that the inspector and I now have sufficient information to enable us to solve this case. To start with, I would ask you, Mr Fortesque to examine this pair of gloves." The constable produced the soiled gloves uncovered by Henry Parks. Fortesque took them gingerly, holding them at arm's length.

"Are these your gloves, Mr Fortesque?" The inspector asked.

"These garments are filthy, Inspector," the hapless butler replied. "I can envisage no circumstance under which a pair of my gloves would degenerate to such a deplorable state."

"Yes, but I would ask you to imagine the garments laundered, starched and pressed to your impeccable standard. In that case, would you say that these gloves might have originated from your glove drawer?"

"It is possible," the butler replied.

"Let me put it this way," Soames interjected. "Is there anyone else in the household who uses gloves of this type?"

"No one."

"And do you accept then that these gloves originated from your supply?"

"If you say so, sir." Fortesque returned the soiled gloves to the constable.

"Very well. I can tell you all," Soames said with a flourish, "that whoever poisoned his lordship's dog did so with the aid of these gloves. Indeed, since the discovery of these gloves it is clear that, not only Mr Catchpole, but *anyone* in the household could have arranged for the poisoning of the beet that killed the dog."

"And may we take it that whoever that was also committed the murders of Betteridge and my brother?" Rebecca asked.

"You may," Soames replied. He turned his attention back to Fortesque. "While we are on the subject, perhaps you would be so kind as to remove your gloves, Mr Fortesque."

Fortesque did so and handed the gloves to Soames.

"Thank you," said Soames. "Now please show everyone the backs of your hands."

There was an audible gasp from everyone present. Fortesque carried the unicorn tattoo on the back of his right hand.

"You carry the tattoo," I said in astonishment.

"Yes," Fortesque replied, "as did his lordship."

"The old duke," Soames added.

"Please explain the significance of the tattoo, Mr Fortesque," said the inspector.

"The Ancient Eclectic International Order of the Unicorn was founded many centuries ago. I believe it originated in the time of St Joan of Arc –"

Soames shook his head. "Earlier than that, much earlier."

"His lordship joined during the period of his diplomatic service in India and I joined shortly thereafter."

"And you, Catchpole?" the inspector enquired.

"I joined in prison," Catchpole replied. "It was the one thing that saved me."

"How so?" Soames prompted.

"His lordship represented my case to the parole board. He used his influence to arrange my parole and when I was released he took me into his employ. God knows where I would be today if it had not been for his intervention."

"And you attribute his intervention entirely to your membership of the AEIOU?"

"Beyond question, sir. AEIOU members stand by one another. It is part of the oath of membership."

Soames turned back to the butler. "So, Mr Fortesque, you, the duke and Catchpole were all sworn members of this organisation. But young Michael, the duke's son was not."

"That is correct. He understood nothing of the oath of loyalty sworn in brotherhood. He would have dismissed me and perhaps Catchpole as well – if he had lived."

"I think we should take some refreshments at this juncture," Soames said. "Morgan, if you would be so kind."

Morgan pulled the bell pull.

"Speaking of dismissals," said Soames, "I understand that the young duke intended to dismiss you, Mr Parks and to make Betteridge head gardener in your place."

"That may be, but as I told you earlier, Mr Soames, I would not have allowed such a thing to happen." Parks stood up as he spoke, his face reddening with anger.

"And how would you have prevented it?" Soames asked. But there was no answer from Parks.

"Our investigations have revealed that you, Miss de Farr had an inappropriate relationship with the undergardener, Betteridge. And it has been suggested that you might have killed him as a result of a lovers' quarrel."

Rebecca blushed copiously. "I loved him!" She declared. "We had plans to run away together and marry. It is quite preposterous to suggest that I killed Betteridge."

"And your brother? Perhaps you killed him for his inheritance?" Inspector Morgan interjected.

"Never!" She responded, and fell silent.

There was a knock at the door, the constable opened it and Gladys appeared carrying a large silver tray of tea and scones. She placed the tray on a small table and turned to leave.

"Gladys, while you are there, you might confirm for us that you spent last night with your lover, Mr. Catchpole," said Soames.

"Yes, sir. That is correct."

"And the evening when Betteridge was murdered, Mr. Catchpole was where?"

"He was with me, sir."

"And the morning when his lordship's dog was poisoned?"

"He was with me on all three occasions, sir."

"You realise that the inspector and his constable are just about to make an arrest." Soames said. "If you are lying, you may be found complicit in all of these crimes."

"Mr Catchpole was with me, sir, on all three occasions, I swear it."

"Very well." Soames turned to where Catchpole sat by the window. "Mr Catchpole, I believe the case against you is irrefutable. First, the dog was poisoned by a beet which his lordship should have eaten and using a toxin from one of your venomous reptiles. Second, you carry the unicorn tattoo and both of the murder victims were slain with the unicorn statuette. Third, you are reported as having had a violent argument with Betteridge on the day before he was killed. Fourth, you knew that the young duke hated you and was going to dismiss you from the household and fifth, you have a criminal record and have served a term of imprisonment for an earlier murder."

"But I am guilty of none of these crimes." Catchpole protested. He leapt to his feet, a wild look in his eyes. Constable Longneck stepped forward and held up a warning hand. Catchpole slumped back into his chair.

"If it were not for the alibi provided by Gladys, here, you would already be rotting in a cell at the police station." Soames turned back to the maid again. "I ask you again, Gladys, do you still stand by your statement that Catchpole was with you on all three occasions?"

There was a long pause. All present looked at Gladys. She seemed to quiver all over, then her body shook and she burst into tears. "I lied!" She wailed. "I'm sorry, sirs. He threatened me. He said that I had to lie to save him. He said if I didn't lie he would kill me too."

Catchpole sprang to his feet again. "This is nonsense!" he shouted. "What are you saying, Gladys?"

"Please sit quietly," the constable said.

Catchpole remained standing and the constable took up a position directly behind him, wrist-bracelets at the ready.

"So Catchpole was not with you when these crimes were committed?" Inspector Morgan said to the maid.

Gladys shook her head. Her ringlets flashed in the lamplight.

– 10 –

"In that case," said the inspector, "I arrest you, Gladys Abbott for the murders of Benjamin Betteridge, under-gardener, and Michael de Farr, twelfth duke of Bish-op-Salford."

Gladys stared at him in amazement. Constable Long-neck stepped around the footman and took firm hold of Gladys's arm and shoulder. There was uproar in the room. All of the others who were seated – me included – rose from their seats.

"You are arresting the maid?" I cried. "What madness is this? Soames ..."

Soames raised his hands to re-establish a measure of calm. "Let me explain."

We resumed our seats.

"Ladies and gentlemen," he said. "Meet Gladys Abbott, previously Gladys Monk, daughter of Albert and Mary Monk. Do you admit this, Gladys?"

Gladys scowled at him.

Soames continued: "You will remember that Mary Monk was murdered and Albert Monk, her husband was executed for her murder. Some time later, this man, Catchpole confessed to the crime and was sentenced, not to the gallows, but to life imprisonment. He was released on parole after serving just twelve years of his sentence, thanks to the intervention of his lordship the duke. Gladys took a position in the duke's household intent on wreaking terrible revenge, not just on Catchpole, the murderer, as she saw it, of both her parents, but also on the duke who intervened to have him released and then provided him with employment.

"Her plan was to have a great injustice righted by killing the duke and framing Catchpole for the crime. It was her intention that Catchpole would be executed for a murder that he did not commit, just as her father had been."

Again there was pandemonium, and again Soames called for quiet. "Unfortunately, her first two attempts at killing the young duke failed. Betteridge and the duke's dog suffered the consequences of those failures. She finally succeeded last night and having created a number of clues pointing to Catchpole, she then provided him with an alibi. It was her intention to break down under questioning – as she did here today. It was all an act, one which she expected would finally seal Catchpole's fate and complete her evil plan."

"But Soames," I protested later, "how on Earth did you deduce all of this from the facts available?"

"Well, her name was a major clue. Abbott is not much removed from Monk, after all. And it was clear to me that, while she was providing false alibis for Catchpole, she was also creating alibis for herself."

"So once she confessed that the alibi was false, she was actually incriminating herself?"

"Precisely, Wilson. Then there was the murder weapon. You will recall that I found it here on the mantle. I ask you, who but a female domestic would place an ornament back where it belongs after using it commit murder?"

"Who indeed, Soames?"

"It is back in its place again. Would you care to examine it?"

I did as he suggested, but could see nothing remarkable in the statuette.

"Take a look at the mantle, Wilson. Notice the complete absence of dust. Who but a housemaid would take the trouble to dust the mantle before replacing the statuette?"

"And what of the old duke?" I asked "Did she murder him too?"

"I doubt it, Wilson. She must have intended to slay him for the part he played in her family's affairs, but I believe the old man died of natural causes before she could act against him."

"So she turned her revenge on his only son?"

"Elementary, my dear Wilson."

"All the same," I said, "an autopsy on the old duke's body would be advisable."

"I think not, Wilson. After all, as a wise man once said: 'Let sleeping dukes lie.' "

UNCLE TOM

First published in Noir Nation 3, 2013 and by JJ Toner Publishing, 2015

It was like watching a film. One of those sexy continental films, only without the subtitles. Without sound, even. She was no looker, but she had a figure like a ripe pear. Small, firm breasts and generous hips. A natural redhead with long, wavy hair, her face a freckled landscape.

The boy was plug-ugly. Short with bandy legs and thin as a knife, like a jockey. Looking at him you'd think he must have been thrown from a horse, the way his nose was squashed and splayed across his face.

I knew what people would think — what they'd call me — if they found out, but if the young lovers couldn't be bothered to draw their curtains why should I feel guilty? And anyway, my name's not Tom, it's Sebastian.

A quick check of their discarded mail revealed her name. Chastity! That made me laugh. If the moniker was intended to protect her against her own biological urges it was a spectacular failure. She'd fallen, and probably to the first serious temptation that came along.

Each morning at 7:45, as I prepared to open the shop, I'd see her heading out alone toward the centre of town. The boy would sleep on close to midday. He'd leave the flat in the afternoon and as dusk fell they would return together laden with bags of groceries. She did the cooking. Thirty minutes it took her to make a meal that they'd eat in fifteen before picking up their love-making where they'd left off. Every day the same routine. You could set your watch by it.

All the action was in their living room. My bedroom is on the third floor, one floor higher than theirs, giving me an uninterrupted view. As long as I left the light off and kept my chair positioned back in the shadows, they had no inkling they were being watched, but still it was a bit of a mystery why they never used the bedroom, where the curtains were always drawn.

The nearest street light had been broken for a year or more, my complaints to Dublin City Council falling on deaf ears. Most of the illumination came from their TV, which was always on — not that the youngsters ever watched it — and there were moonlit nights.

The main object in my view was a couch, vaguely blue in colour. To the naked eye the grime on the window opposite was every bit as effective as lace curtains, but my powerful binoculars cut through all the visual interference and transported me into the room with them.

They made love on the couch sometimes, but mostly on the floor. In reality there wasn't that much to see, but my imagination was a dragon feeding on morsels — squirming, rhythmical movements under a dark blanket; a bare arm or the girl's face caught in a moonbeam; the occasional tantalizing flash of the boy's bare buttocks.

***

It was early spring when I first noticed them. All through spring and into summer I watched them. Then, in the height of summer, he came into the shop. I was in my cage serving one of my regulars, number 533, a single mother hauling an old coal scuttle. Not much call for coal scuttles nowadays, but I gave her a fiver for the brass. Next up was 139, a middle-aged man who pawned the same watch every month.

"See you in four weeks, Uncle," 139 said cheerily on his way out. So far, I'd seen that watch seventeen times, and sixteen times he'd redeemed it.

The boy was next in line. He gave his name, his address the house across the road. I entered his details in the book and he presented me with a pair of silver candlesticks, plain and modern, untraceable.

After that first visit he came into the shop about twice a month, with silver, mostly. His name was Jason. He tried to offload items of jewellery on me a few times, turning his soft eyes up at me, spinning unlikely yarns about recently deceased country relatives. I sent him packing, of course; that sort of shite I've heard a thousand times, and I know a night worker when I see one. Some of it was good stuff, too.

What Chastity saw in him I could not imagine. Up close he was like a troll. She must have known hundreds of boys. What was it about this particular unremarkable boy in baggy pants and threadbare sweater that turned her head? He made her laugh. It was laughter all the way when they were together. Was that enough? Soft eyes, a flattened nose and a killer sense of humour? Was that all it took to wipe out every sensible word of caution from fifteen years at a convent school?

***

A couple of weeks into the autumn they disappeared. I sat in my room until well after dark but they never showed. Every bit as disappointed as an abandoned lover, my heart bled. The next night was the same story, and the night after that. The sense of loss was overpowering. At first I was bewildered, then annoyed, then enraged. I felt cheated, betrayed. Reason abandoned me. I smashed a glass of beer against the bedroom wall and then spent an hour hunting for band aids and cleaning up the mess.

I closed the shop early, stuffed my pockets from the till, and walked round to Feathers nightclub in Dame Street. Nursing a bottle of cheap wine, I watched a succession of women in scanty clothing dance around a pole. Close enough to the stage to smell their sweat and pheromones, I should have been aroused, but I felt nothing. Later, one of the women led me to an alcove and did a solo dance in my lap, her silicon breasts like two huge moons orbiting inches from my head. I could barely keep my eyes open.

Picking out the best-looking girl in the place, I invited her to sit at my table. A marginal bottle of Champagne set me back €75, and the girl spoke seductively as she drank it. I did my best to respond to her advances, but my heart wasn't in it. No teenager was ever so love-sick as I was that night.

When the decision point arrived, I made my excuses and hurried home. The kids' flat was empty, dark and cold as a tomb.

***

I kept a vigil in my room every night for a week. Those nights were bad, the days not much better. Like an automaton, I went through the motions, greeting my regular customers with a pasty smile through the grille. One woman (474) offered me a top hat. I gave her seven euro. For a top hat! No wonder her eyes lit up in surprise. She had her toddler in tow. Maybe that was why I was so *flaithiúlach*.

Then one night, the couple reappeared. The TV was switched on and they resumed their old routine. My heart did a back-flip.

I watched every move, but not simply as a voyeur. Not anymore. I still got a sexual thrill from the show, but there was a deeper emotional bond there as well. These kids had become part of my life, their lives precious to me. I felt connected to them and I was consumed by a need for more information about their relationship. How deep were their feelings for one another? Was this a passing fancy or something that would lead to a lifelong commitment? I could see their lips move as they spoke, but I'd never learnt to lip-read. I reached out with my mind, attempting to interpret their body language. Was her laugh genuine or was she growing tired of his endless supply of old jokes? What about his shrug, was it a gesture of affection or did it hide a deeper indifference?

Night after night I tossed about in the sheets for hours, my mind in turmoil. I wondered if the boy was faithful to her or if he might be seeing other girls behind her back. Were they in love or was it purely a physical relationship based on carnal lusts? Was his love-making tender, giving, or rough, self-gratifying, inconsiderate? And so on. An abundance of questions, but no answers.

A week went by. The hours of daylight were spent shut up in my cage dispensing paltry sums of money in exchange for worthless tat. Early evenings were show time, all the time my curiosity eating me from inside like a worm in the gut, driving a wedge between me and my sanity.

I resolved to do something about it. "Tomorrow," I declared.

***

The next morning Manliffe turned up unannounced.

Manliffe is a wrecking ball, forty-something, six foot four with a body frame like a double-decker bus.

Before I could recover from one of his bear hugs he was through the counter flap and heading for the kitchen, sending my lamp standard into a spin.

"Had breakfast yet, Uncle?" he called out.

I righted the lamp and followed him up the stairs.

He poked his bald head into the fridge and pulled out a carton of milk. "There's not much in here. Haven't you been shopping?"

"Not recently, no. Look here, Manliffe," I said, "you might have given me some warning."

He turned, splaying his enormous hands in a gesture of confused enquiry, my milk dribbling between his Stonehenge teeth. "Mammy rang. Didn't you get her messages?"

I grabbed the milk carton from him. "No, I've been busy."

"Doing what?" He flashed a milk-moustached grin at me.

I handed him a fifty. "Why don't you go and get some food for the both of us?"

He grinned some more. "Can I buy wagon-wheels, Uncle?"

For some reason wagon-wheels were unavailable in Wexford, where he lived, and he had developed a fondness bordering on addiction for the things on previous visits.

"Yes, now go. And don't call me Uncle. I've told you a hundred times, I'm not your uncle, I'm your second cousin."

"I can't call you Second Cousin, Uncle," he said, elbowing his way along the corridor to the front door and out into the street.

"Call me Sebastian," I shouted after him, righting my lamp standard for a second time.

While he was gone I spent a frantic half hour hiding away anything breakable or remotely fragile. Porcelain and glass, musical instruments, radios, a couple of TVs — anything with moving parts. I had a closet full of things he'd broken on previous visits, and there had been a few embarrassing — and expensive — episodes when customers had returned to redeem stuff that Manliffe had chipped or broken.

I sorted out the back bedroom for him and tried to persuade him to go to bed early. Of course that was never going to happen; he hadn't seen me for a year and he had a lot to talk about.

Two o'clock in the morning, Manliffe ran out of things to say and retired to his room. The flat across the road was dark, as I knew it would be, but I caught a glimpse of Jason, dressed from head to feet in dark clothing, heading out for his night's work.

***

Things settled into a sort of uneasy rhythm. Manliffe took my place in the cage while I busied myself in the back room valuing the stock and selling some of it over the phone. I made quite a bit of money during the first week, as I usually did when Manliffe was there to man the cage. With his throaty laugh and the titters of the women, the ambient sound level in the shop rose.

The evenings were a little tricky. In previous years, Manliffe and I would spend time together watching television or playing cards before retiring to our respective rooms; this year, I had to fake a strange malady that necessitated my going to bed early every night.

Half-way through week two, Manliffe discovered my secret. Dusk was falling and I was thinking about sneaking away to watch the show when he excused himself and went upstairs to use the john.

A few moments later I heard a yelp from upstairs. "Uncle, come quick. You won't believe the view from this window!"

I charged up the stairs.

Manliffe's huge form filled my bedroom window, the binoculars firmly attached to his skull. And he had the light on.

I groaned, switched off the light and screamed at him, "Get away from the window!" He looked at me in bewilderment. "They'll see you, you great oaf."

"Oh, right," he said, backing away from the window.

But it was too late. One glance across the street told me that the young couple had seen Manliffe at the window and retired to the privacy of their bedroom. Tearing the binoculars from his grasp, I shoved Manliffe into his own room, and slammed the door.

"How long have you been watching them, Uncle?" he called out. I could hear his ear-to-ear grin through the door.

I sat on my bed, my head reeling. The show was over. The loss felt like an amputation. Not only that, but I had no idea how Jason would react. I could imagine him exacting some sort of retribution. He might get violent, and he was a lot younger than me. What really made me sweat, though, was that I had laid myself open to blackmail. If the holy Joes of the parish heard what I'd been doing my feet wouldn't touch the ground. They'd run me out of town like a bad smell. I might even have to leave the country. My business would be ruined.

***

That was a bad night. Manliffe refused to settle, firing a hundred quick-fire questions at me. I tried to placate him with wagon-wheels, but he would have none of it. He called me some horrible names. By sunrise we were both strung out like matching g-strings on a washing line.

By 8 am, Manliffe was in the kitchen and the shop was full of the sounds and smells of frying bacon. I opened the front door to find Jason waiting on the doorstep schlepping a large carry-all.

"Got some good stuff for you here, Uncle." The expression on his face was difficult to read.

I grabbed one of the bag's handles and we hauled it in together. It was heavy. We dropped it on the counter top, and I looked inside. There was an assortment of silver, half a dozen small bronze figurines, some rings, and a heap of jewellery.

I went through the haul. The silver wasn't worth much. There was some gold, mostly low-grade stuff. A lot of it was engraved, which meant it would have to be melted down. As for the rest, there was no way I could shift any of it. The figurines were exquisite. They were obviously from a single collection, and I knew they'd be hotter than Tabasco. Just touching them gave me the shivers. Likewise the jewellery. Some of it was high quality, someone's family heirlooms, old as Mother Reilly and probably featured on police notice boards all over the country.

Jason squinted at me, tip-tapping the floor with his foot. "How much for the lot?" The coming exchange was taking shape in my mind. He had me over a barrel.

"I want you to understand—" I began.

"Spare me the sob story, Uncle. Cut to the bottom line."

"I'll take the gold and silver for the metal, but not the jewellery. And these bronze figurines must be red hot."

"You owe me, Uncle. Me and my girl both." He tucked his fingers into the pockets of his jeans. He was wearing Mexican heels, and his legs looked bandier that usual. It was easy to imagine a broken-backed horse tied up outside.

"For the silver and the gold, I can give you six hundred."

"And for the rest?"

"I'm sorry." I gave him my wounded puppy look; the gentle head shake, the hooded sympathetic eyes, that said: 'You know I'd help you if it was humanly possible, but I'd be slitting my own throat.'

He watched me for a few moments, running his eyes up and down my body like a crocodile contemplating a meal.

"I'm disappointed in you, Uncle. I reckon all this stuff must be worth at least twenty grand."

The blood rushed from my face; my legs turned to rubber. "Twenty grand? You must be mad!"

He folded his skinny arms. "Give me a fair price and we'll call it quits."

"A thousand?" I said.

He sidled over and laughed in my face. Up close, he had the flat-nosed look of a bull, stray whiskers and all. "The figurines alone are worth five times that." He snorted.

"Maybe, but there's no way I could dispose of them. I'm not that way connected."

He moved even closer, pressing me against the counter top. I could have pushed him away; I was three inches taller and I had a good 70 pound weight advantage, but I didn't want to antagonise him further. My neck began to ache.

"I'll do what I can," I said.

"Haven't I seen you going to Mass in the Franciscan church?" He sneered. "What would the good brothers think if I told them what you've been up to?"

"You've made your point."

"And the congregation, what would they think?"

"Okay, Jason. I said I'll do what I can."

"You'll take the figurines?" He leaned in closer. "You'll take it all?"

"Yes, yes! I'll take it all." He stepped back.

Massaging my neck, I succumbed to a coughing fit. I was sweating, and my stomach was doing somersaults. When I could talk I said, "Leave it with me."

"No way, Uncle." He started throwing the jewels back into the bag. "I'm not letting any of this gear out of my sight."

I said, "How am I going to sell it without showing it around?"

"I'm coming with you, Uncle. We'll do it together."

"Okay, meet me here tomorrow afternoon. Two o'clock." The last thing I needed was the little toe-rag peering over my shoulder, but how could I refuse?

Jason gave me a last, lingering look before hauling the bag out of the shop. As soon as he'd gone, Manliffe put in an appearance.

"What did he want?"

"Where were you when I needed you?" I said.

"Little pipsqueak like that? Why didn't you squash him like a bug?"

"You know why, Manliffe."

***

That evening, as Manliffe and I shared a meal, he asked if I'd had any direct contact with the girl.

"What sort of contact?" I snapped.

"I wondered if you've ever met her, spoken to her. You know. Contact."

"No," I gave him the full glowering eyebrows effect, "and that's never going to happen now, is it? I don't know why I have to put up with you every year."

He pouted. "You used to say I was welcome, Uncle."

"You're a walking disaster. Not only do you break all my stuff, but now you've ruined everything."

He gave me his baby seal look. "I'm sorry, Uncle."

"And don't call me Uncle."

He waddled over to the fridge, took out a wagon-wheel and unwrapped it. He broke it in two and offered me half.

"I don't want it."

He stuffed both halves into his huge mouth. It was a while before he spoke again. Then he came out with, "You should ask to join in."

"Join in? What d'you mean, join in?"

"You know, get to know them and wangle an invitation to... join in."

I blew a fuse. "That's a disgusting suggestion, Manliffe."

"Sorry, Uncle."

I tried to explain the subtlety of my relationship with Jason and Chastity. Manliffe looked at me blankly.

***

The next morning was a Saturday. My mood was sombre, deflated. Facing a bleak future of adult movies and trips to the nightclub, I resolved to approach the girl and break the ice. Perhaps I could play a new, positive role in their lives, watching over them, keeping them from harm. I could advise them on financial matters, let them have small loans to tide them over difficult times.

A couple of my regulars were in. A young single mother, 667, offered me an electric kettle. As I recorded the transaction in the book, she gave me a crooked smile and said, "Where's the big fella, today?"

I didn't reply. My mind was elsewhere. Perhaps I could persuade Jason to give up his life of crime, find a proper job, marry Chastity and settle down.

"Where is he?" she said again.

"Who, Manliffe? He's in the back somewhere."

I would urge them strongly to save enough for a deposit for their first house. And my experience would be invaluable when it came to selecting a suitable property. I could visit them at Christmas. Buy presents for their little ones. A boy and a girl. Perhaps a second boy that they might name Sebastian after their benevolent uncle.

I called Manliffe to take over at the counter.

Wrapped in my new avuncular persona, I hurried round to the Franciscan church under a cold, overcast sky. Turn and turn about, the doors of the confession boxes swung open and closed in a steady rhythm. Business was brisk. When my turn came I made a full and frank confession to the priest. Afterwards, free of all my sins, cocooned in a righteous glow, I stepped from the church into the light. The streets were bathed in warm sunlight; the clouds had dissipated. Feeling light as a bird, I skipped home, humming to myself.

"Hello Uncle." I'd forgotten how harsh Jason's voice could be. He was waiting by the car with his bag of booty.

It was after two o'clock. I unlocked the car and we lifted the bag into the boot. Jason took the front passenger seat.

"Give me a minute," I said, stepping into the shop.

Manliffe was on duty, looking like an overfed parrot stuffed into a budgie's cage.

"I have to go out. Mind the store while I'm gone."

"How long for?"

"A couple of hours. Three at the most."

"Right ho, Uncle." There was a strange glint in Manliffe's eyes.

***

As we headed off toward my first contact, Jason settled back in his seat. "I've been thinking, Uncle. I reckon we can help each other."

"I've been thinking the same thing, Jason." My cheeks still glowed from my recent epiphany. "You know I've grown fond of you, of the pair of you." I glanced at him and he gave me a crooked grin. "I don't mean like that. I mean you're like members of my family, now."

"Family."

"I'd like you to think of me as someone you can call on, someone you can confide in. I'd like you to think of me as a friend. I can help in all sorts of ways."

He pulled a battered cigarette from somewhere and began to search his pockets for a light.

"I'm concerned for your future, Jason. You and I both know where you'll end up if you carry on as you have been. It can only be a matter of time before you're caught and they lock you up."

"You reckon?"

"I'm sure of it. I know how much you and Chastity love each other, and I'm sure you'd like to settle down and build a life together, get married, maybe start a—"

"Now hold on there, Uncle."

"Okay, so maybe marriage is not in your plans yet, but I'd like to see you get a proper job, save up for your own house."

I paused for a reaction from Jason, but he was fully occupied lighting his cigarette.

"I can see a rosy future for both of you, if you had a proper job, a small house, a secondhand car, a couple of kids..."

"You see us as Mr and Mrs Everyone? Who's going to give *me* a job?"

"There must be lots of opportunities out there for someone like you, Jason. You're young, healthy, intelligent. I'm sure we can find a job for you."

"We?"

"I can help you. That's what I've been trying to say. I can help in so many ways."

"Like a real uncle." He grinned.

"If you'll let me, yes."

***

First stop was a council house in Finglas. I won't mention his name, but this guy is seriously heavy. He's easily the best fence in the city — in the country — and I knew he'd take all the cool stuff off my hands, and maybe give me some ideas where I could shift the hotter items. There were a few hairy moments while I explained who my companion was. As I said, Otto's a heavy-hitter, not someone to be messed with, but he accepted Jason on face value. Luckily Jason's face looked the part.

We weren't disappointed. He took the metals and some of the rings and gave me a couple of useful leads. Jimmy The Lisp was in the market for individual stones, and he had the equipment to pop them from their settings.

Back in the car, Jason held out his hand and clicked his fingers. I handed him the cash I'd got from the hard man and started the engine. We headed for Jimmy's place.

Jimmy took most of the jewellery, leaving us with a few rings and the remains of the jewels. I showed him the bronze figurines.

Jimmy whistled. "Nice pieces," he lisped. "Sizzling hot, but."

"Maybe a little warm," I said.

"Warm? They're radio-fucken-active!" said Jimmy.

"Any idea where we might shift them?" Jason said.

Jimmy wrote an address on a piece of paper and handed it to me. "Probably your only hope."

I thanked him and we left.

Again, Jason relieved me of Jimmy's cash. "Where to next, Uncle?" he said.

I read the address on the piece of paper. "Enniskillen. We should go home, start again in the morning." It was getting late.

"I don't think so, Uncle. Let's keep going until we've shifted the lot."

I filled the petrol tank at a filling station and we headed north.

Jason fell asleep. After about fifty miles, he woke up again, rubbed his eyes, yawned and said, "Where are we?"

"We've just crossed the border."

He found a second battered cigarette and lit it. "I'd like to propose a business partnership, Uncle."

"Okay. What did you have in mind?"

"You find me the marks and I turn them over. Then you fence the goods. How does that sound?"

"What? You want me to identify premises for you to burgle." I couldn't believe what he'd said.

"That's it."

"How do I do that, exactly?"

"You must know lots of well-heeled people. All you have to do is find out when they're planning to go on holiday and let me know. I do the business, and then you fence the goods. Between us we could make a good living. Chute, we're already partners, you and me."

I took a deep breath. The boy's thinking was about as screwed up as it could be. "Didn't you hear anything I said back in Dublin?"

He shrugged his shoulders, turned the radio on, and the discussion ended there.

The rest of our journey was a nightmare. The Enniskillen contact was not at home when we called and we had to spend the night in a B&B. The southern reg number on my car drew a lot of unwanted attention. We found it the next morning parked where I'd left it, but facing the wrong way, and minus its four wheels.

Being Sunday we couldn't find anyone to help us. We had to spend a second night in the B&B. On the Monday, we got the car wheels replaced, completed our business with the Enniskillen fence and set off for home.

We covered thirty miles in silence. Jason's eyes were closed and I had just about decided he was asleep when he spoke. "I knew you wouldn't go for it."

"Go for what?"

"My partnership idea."

"I'm a law-abiding citizen."

"I have another proposition for you, Uncle."

"Nothing to do with breaking and entering, I hope."

"How would it be if the show started again?"

I turned to face him. The car wobbled on the road. "I want no more of that, Jason. Haven't you been listening to me? You and Chastity are family to me, now."

"Yeah, I know, but how would it be if I got her to do things?"

"What d'you mean, 'do things'?"

"Whatever you want, Uncle. For a fee. You tell me what you'd like to see and I'll arrange it."

"You're not serious."

"Sure. Why not?"

"How would Chastity feel about that?"

"I've sounded her out already. She's game."

"You're sure?"

"Sure, I'm sure. The girl's a simple soul. I'm her whole world. She'll do anything I tell her to do."

My knees turned to water and the sleeping dragon that was my imagination opened one bleary eye.

***

By the time we got home, Jason was nearly €2,000 and £600 richer. I was lighter by the cost of food and accommodation, the petrol, 4 new wheels and the garage charges, a little over €1,700. I still had the figurines. We hadn't managed to shift them and I'd agreed to pay Jason another €400 for them.

It was midday. 139 was on the doorstep looking pained. When he saw me, a look of relief washed over his face. He thrust some money into my fist. "It wasn't easy, but I managed to raise the cash again. Why is the shop locked? It's not usually locked at this time."

I opened the door. The standard lamp was stretched out like a corpse on the hall floor. The cage was empty. I gave the man his watch and he left. Then I checked the book. In the time that we'd been away Manliffe had taken in a total of five items. No new customers had registered. Saturday's my busiest day. I normally take in ten items an hour on Saturdays.

I checked Manliffe's room. His stuff was gone.

Exhausted from the stress of the trip and all the driving, I climbed the stairs towards my bed. My cash resources were depleted, I was left with a bagful of bronze with a half-life of twenty years, and Manliffe had been doing his best to put me out of business while I was away.

There was a knock on the door. I ignored it. Another knock, louder, thumping, more insistent. I opened the bedroom window and shouted down. "We're closed. Come back in the morning."

"It's me. Let me in."

I went down, opened the door and let Jason in.

"She's locked me out." The usual cocky expression on his face was gone. He looked like a toad in a desert.

"Don't you have a key?"

"She's changed the lock."

Jason ran up the stairs. I found him at my bedroom window peering through my binoculars.

"What can you see?"

"Nothing. The TV's on. No sign of Chastity. Wait. There she is. She's waving. No, scrub that. She's giving me the finger."

"Who's she with?"

"I can't see anyone else. She's eating something. Something chocolate. Looks like one of those – what're they called?"

"Wagon wheels," I said.

A CLEAN GETAWAY

Fresh out of training college, it was PC Gerry Purcell's second day on the job. Inspector Malone was attending a conference in the city, so the desk sergeant had to find him something to do. Gerry spent the morning sorting index cards into alphabetical order. At lunchtime he wandered into town, sat alone on a park bench and ate his egg sandwiches. The warm afternoon sun on his face, he closed his eyes.

When he was a boy, Gerry often dreamt that he could fly. All he had to do was lean forward into the breeze and he would rise up off the ground. Once he was airborne, he could hover over one spot or accelerate away and up into the clouds.

When he returned to the station the desk sergeant could think of nothing else for Gerry to do, so he gave him a newspaper to read. The station was quieter than the morgue.

***

The gang hit the bank two minutes from closing time. Driscoll took out the security man. Jimmy 'the face' positioned himself where his sawn-off covered the entire room. Mad Mungo did the talking. He had just the right deep flint-chip voice and the attitude for the job.

"Everybody on the floor. Faces down."

Mungo picked out the youngest, best-looking teller, gave her a canvas bag and ordered her to fill it. Jimmy was scratching his face. His woollen mask always irritated his scar. Driscoll grinned behind his mask. Nothing made his day like a good bank job and the young bank teller filled her white sweater to perfection.

Suddenly, Jimmy swivelled and let fly with both barrels, tearing a huge hole in a partition wall.

"Christ, Jimmy. What was that for?" Driscoll shouted.

Everybody's ears were ringing.

In answer to Driscoll's question, a manager-type wearing a suit emerged through the hole with his hands on his head and lay down on the floor with the others. Jimmy reloaded the sawn-off.

Mungo shouted, "The alarm's gone off," and they all stopped to listen. There was a bell ringing outside – faint, but insistent.

Driscoll grabbed the bag and shouted, "Asses in gear, lads."

Mungo called out in a gruff singsong voice, "Thank you all for banking with us. Have a nice day."

They ran. Whipping off their balaclavas, they threw themselves into the back seat of the waiting BMW.

***

Alone in the back room of the police station, PC Purcell put down the tabloid and closed his eyes. Soon, he was gliding along six inches above the city pavements. He lifted his eyes to the sky and rose into the air, levelling off just above the tops of the houses.

The door crashed open and Inspector Malone burst into the station. "Where's the new man?" he shouted.

The desk sergeant's mouth was full. He nodded toward the inner office.

"Come on, son," said the inspector. "Time to get your feet wet."

Inspector Malone and PC Purcell ran outside and jumped into a squad car, its engine running.

***

"How much did we get, boss?" said Gordo the getaway driver.

"Fifty, sixty grand," said Driscoll.

Sitting by the window rubbing the scar on his face, Jimmy let out one of his Yee-haaas that rattled everyone's nerves.

Then they heard a siren. A blue light was flashing in their rear window, and Gordo went into action.

***

The BMW hit the airport highway doing a ton plus. Ahead of them a small red Nissan was overtaking an articulated lorry. Gordo had to reduce speed. The police driver moved up level, boxing them in.

"Bastards," roared Mad Mungo.

PC Purcell looked across at the BMW and made eye contact with a middle-aged man with an ugly red scar that ran down from his right eye across his mouth.

"Get us out of here," Driscoll roared.

Gordo threw the car onto the hard shoulder, and floored the accelerator. The police car followed. Just as the police car drew level with the Nissan the Nissan driver swerved to the right and caught the squad car broadside. The heavy squad car rocked on its rear wheels, then, as if lifted by an invisible hand, it rose into the air.

There was silence. In slow motion, the squad car sailed over the top of a hedge. For one long second before the squad car began to spin, before it hit the ground, before it bust into a ball of flames, just for one long second PC Gerry Purcell was flying.

MURDER PLAN B

Harry Schneider was an Automobile Marketing Consultant, or so it said on his gold edged business card. Actually, he was a used car salesman, although he preferred to describe the cars he sold as "previously enjoyed". He lived with his wife and two kids in Yuma County AZ, and like millions of his neighbors, and most of his friends, his life was uncomplicated, if a little dull.

Melissa, his wife, was a little older than Harry. In her youth she had been a looker of ample proportions, smooth and streamlined like the Lincoln Continental. Now pushing forty-something, she was well built in the way that the 1975 Cadillac was—every curve over-accentuated and with overflowing upholstery.

Harry and Melissa served together for a short time as deputies in the sheriff's department before they married, and it was there that they met and fell in love.

Some women lose interest in men in early middle age, but not Melissa. Sexually, she was as fresh as the day she left high school. If anything, her sexual appetite had increased with the passing years. And this was where the problem lay. Harry was a passionate enough man, but usually only on Saturday nights or early in the morning about once each month. Also, his timing was invariably poor. It had always been poor, and his attempts at lovemaking had always been furtive, groping, uninformed and far, far too quick.

He was very fond of Melissa, and she knew that, of course. She understood that it was his passion for her that prevented him from postponing his sexual fulfillment and satisfying her deep need for slow lovemaking.

The upshot of this state of affairs was that, from about the second year of their marriage, Melissa had engaged in affairs, mostly with married men in and around Yuma, Phoenix and other cities in Arizona, as well as a number of adjoining states. Most recently, under the pretext of squash lessons, she had been meeting Lance J. Masiak, the local tennis pro, fifteen years her junior, but with a sexual maturity way beyond his years.

Harry never objected to the high cost of the lessons. He could see how much pleasure she got from them. She would return from the club on Tuesdays and Fridays glowing and walking on air. Once or twice, he suggested taking out joint membership of the club, but Melissa made it a condition that he drop his Thursday night poker sessions, and that was that.

***

Harry enjoyed his job. He was never late for work, kept his paperwork in good order at all times, and was always available for extra duties in the office when the need arose.

His biggest problem was a bright green 1965 Ford Mustang, which had been traded in by a retired hippie about six months earlier. After the garage took possession of the car, it was cleaned thoroughly, right down to the wheel arches, the tires blackened and the chrome polished and it was handed over to Harry to sell. Harry had paid the hippie $3,000 for it, so it was priced on the lot at $7,500. After a couple of months, the Mustang was taken back to the service department for an engine overhaul and marked down to $7,000. Harry tried advertising it in the local press as "buy of the month", but he couldn't shift it. He even advertised it in the national press and one or two specialist auto magazines, but still the old car refused to budge.

One Thursday in November, Harry knocked on Marty Benson's door.

Marty was fifty-something, balding and overweight. He had inherited Benson Autos ten years earlier from his father, whose only claim to fame was that he had imported the first Bugati into the USA in 1932.

"Marty," said Harry, "I'm worried about the Mustang."

"Six months on the lot and already you're worried! Harry, you surprise me." Marty was from a solidly Christian background, but he enjoyed Jewish-American humor.

Harry smiled. Experience had taught him to be wary of Marty, especially when he was being humorous. "I would like to mark it down a notch. I'm sure I could shift it at $6,000."

"Six thousand! A notch? And you paid how much for it? Remind me, Harry."

"Three thousand."

"And did we overhaul the engine? I thought we did, but my mind is playing tricks, maybe."

"Yes, Marty, we did, but ..."

"So what should we allow for the overhaul? Two thousand, maybe? No, let's be generous. Let's say One thousand seven hundred and fifty. And you want to mark it down to six thousand. What percentage profit margin is that, Harry?"

"Erm." Math was not Harry's strongest subject.

"Twenty one percent, Harry. Now, what sort of a profit margin is that?"

"Okay," said Harry.

"Okay? What do you mean, okay? Is it okay to buy scrap iron at automobile prices and sell at bargain basement? Maybe we are running a charity here and nobody told me."

"Okay, so I will leave the price where it is."

"Do I look stupid, Harry? Do I look like I want to let my assets rust on the lot?"

"No ..."

"No. Thank you, Harry." He smiled. "I tell you what, Harry. I'm going to leave this one in your hands entirely. You decide what price to sell it. You decide where to advertise. You decide, and I will back your decisions all the way. Let's make it nice and simple, Harry. Anything above twenty five percent, you can keep. Now that's fair, isn't it?" Harry nodded. "And anything below twenty five percent, you make up out of your wages, okay?"

Harry returned to his own office in a smothered rage and, after some tortuous math, he marked the Mustang down to $6,450. He was sweating as he drove home.

***

Thursday night was poker night. Harry had a cool shower and watched some TV with the kids before setting out for his friend George's house.

George Little was one of Harry's oldest friends. They had met in junior school, but had not become really firm friends until high school, when Harry started to have spectacular success with the girls. George was big and clumsy and not too bright, and he found that his luck with the girls improved beyond his wildest dreams when he and Harry hunted as a pair. After high school, their friendship lapsed for a few years, and then George came to Harry looking for a good used car. Harry obliged and their friendship was reborn.

Father Pat O'Hanlon, the local Catholic curate was the first to arrive. At fifty, he was the oldest of the group. A tall, cheerful Irishman with a colorful past, Father Pat was probably the best poker player of the group, and usually made a modest profit from his Thursday night's work. None of the others ever objected because they knew that the priest used the extra income for charitable works.

Next to arrive was Deputy Sheriff Mort Mooney, followed soon afterwards by Pete Stricker. Pete was an accountant who worked for the local Coca Cola factory. He had a serious shortage of hair on his head and, perhaps in an effort to compensate for his baldness, sported bushy eyebrows and a florid moustache. Pete and Mort were not the best of friends. They were roughly the same age, but had very little else in common apart from their shared interest in body building. Mort's main distinguishing feature was his front teeth, which were splayed, and through which he liked to whistle.

Mike Raymer, the sixth regular poker player was out of town on a fishing trip. Mike was a talented musician and a youth leader. He was highly regarded by all who knew him. He was a clever poker player, much given to strategic bluff during hands with large pots.

Harry was tired. He did not enjoy the poker as much as usual, and by 2.00 a.m. he was twenty-three dollars down on the night.

"I think we should call it a night," said Harry. He stretched and yawned.

The yawn made its way around the table like a baton in a relay race.

"One more hand, lads, okay?" said Father Pat. He was ninety-six dollars up and keen to continue.

Pete checked his watch. "Just one more hand," he said. "I'm meeting Lance Masiak at the tennis club later."

"Isn't it a bit late for tennis lessons, Pete?" said Father Pat.

"He asked me to go over his accounts. The IRS are buzzing him big time."

"What time are you meeting him?" asked Father Pat.

"Two forty-five. There's plenty of time for another hand."

"That's a bit late for tax advice," said Harry. "You sure you don't have a couple girls lined up."

They all sniggered. George fetched another round of beers from the kitchen. Pete dealt the hand.

"I had a call from Masiak the other day," said Mort, whistling between his teeth. "He's been getting anonymous threatening letters."

"Who from?" asked George.

"They weren't signed, George," said Father Pat, patiently.

"What sort of threats, Mort?" said Harry.

"The usual sort. 'You will die' and 'I am coming to get you'." Mort replied.

"Fairly serious stuff," said the priest.

"It wasn't you, Harry, was it?" asked Pete.

"No," said Harry. "What do you mean?"

"Well I mean let's face it you have more cause than most," said Pete with a grin.

"I'm sorry," said Harry. "I'm not with you. I barely know the guy."

"Come on, lads. Are we playing poker or what?" said Father Pat.

"I want Pete to explain what he's getting at." Harry could feel his blood pressure rising.

"Just leave it, Harry. He didn't mean anything," said Father Pat.

Pete looked uncomfortable. He put the cards down.

George said, "Melissa knows him."

"Yes. She has lessons from him," said Harry.

"Yes, but what sort of lessons?" Pete sneered.

Harry stood up. "What the hell are you driving at? Come on, Pete. Spit it out."

Pete looked at Mort. Mort stood up and steered Harry away from the table.

"Now, calm down, Harry. Pete was just kidding."

The last poker hand was abandoned. Harry drove to Murphy's all-night bar and had a couple of stiff Jack Daniels before heading home. Melissa was snoring gently as he slid into bed beside her.

***

The next day was Friday. Harry went to work as usual, and by ten o'clock he had sold the Mustang. Harry was continually amazed at the reasons why people buy cars. In this case, the buyer was a retired spinster school teacher, and she bought it because she liked the color of the upholstery (puce).

Pete Stricker dropped by to ask for advice about his 1980 Jaguar. Harry took it for a spin and advised Pete to hold on to it. "Sporty jalopies like this will be in demand over the next few years," he said.

"Like that Mustang that you had so much trouble getting rid of," jeered Pete.

At ten-thirty, Melissa rang. She was in tears and close to hysteria.

"Harry, I need you," she wailed.

"What's the matter, Honey? Where are you?"

"I'm at the tennis club. Harry, it's Lance."

"Lance? Lance Masiak?"

"Oh Harry. He's ... he's ..."

"He's what, Melissa? Come on, Honey. You're not making sense."

"Oh Harry, Lance is dead," she wailed into the phone.

Harry could get no more sense from her, so he took the morning off and drove to the tennis club.

The sheriff's car was parked outside. There was a small crowd of curious onlookers huddled in the car park, and the front door of the building was cordoned off with yellow tape marked "scene of crime - do not cross".

Near the entrance, Harry caught Mort's eye and Mort allowed him in. He found Melissa sitting in the gymnasium in her squash gear. Her mascara had run down her face in long black streaks.

***

Melissa had found Lance Masiak's body sitting in the corner of a squash court. His head was lowered and his hands lay palms-up by his sides. The rope with which he had been strangled was still wrapped tightly around his neck.

Doctor Feinberg examined the body, and delivered a preliminary verbal report to Sheriff Johnson. "Clearly, he was strangled by that rope. Whoever did it must have been at least as strong as the victim."

"A man?"

"Yes. Definitely not a woman, I'd say. Lance Masiak was an athlete, after all."

"Anything else you can tell me, Doc?"

"Well, look at the bruising on his arms and face, and the rope burn marks on his fingers. I would say he put up quite a struggle."

"And the time of death?" asked the sheriff.

"Difficult to say, Quentin. Some time early this morning. I would guess six to twelve hours. Say, somewhere between midnight and six a.m."

"Can't you narrow it down some more, Doc?" said the sheriff.

"Yes, I should be able to, but I will need to get him back to the surgery to run some tests."

"Right. Thank you, Doc."

***

Back in his office, Sheriff Johnson called Deputy Mort Mooney in for a conference. Mort took a seat and the sheriff buzzed his intercom.

"Yes, Sheriff."

"Hold all calls, Susanne."

"Right, Sheriff."

He turned to Mort. "Okay, Mort, let's go over what we have so far. The victim, Lance J. Masiak, tennis pro—"

"And well-known ladies' man," interrupted Mort.

"... And womanizer, yes. Thirty or thereabouts, I'd say. Athletic. Looked after himself. No sign of any family in the area?"

"None, Sheriff."

"Right, so who would want to kill him?"

"Apart from the anonymous letter writer, you mean?"

"Including the anonymous letter writer."

"Pete Stricker said he had an appointment with him last night. He said he was going to check Masiak's tax returns."

"What time did the game break up?"

"Two o'clock."

"That's a bit late for tax auditing," said the sheriff.

"He said his appointment was for two forty-five."

"Interesting. Was there anything else?"

"Well ..." Mort hesitated.

"Yes, Mort?"

"Well, I mentioned the threatening letters, and Stricker suggested maybe Harry might have written them."

"And why should Harry have written them?"

"Well ... Melissa and Masiak were ..." He gestured and whistled in explanation.

"Hmm. I see. So how did Harry react?"

"He was furious. Harry didn't seem to be aware of Melissa's ..."

"Peccadilloes?" suggested the sheriff. "Perhaps it's just as well. If Harry Schneider killed every man in this town who's had an affair with Melissa, there wouldn't be enough left to make up a volleyball team. Okay, what else do we have, Mort?"

"Not a lot, Sheriff."

"Where did Masiak live?"

"Apartment twelve, Jefferson House. He lived alone."

"Okay, Mort, I'll talk to Pete Stricker and check out Masiak's apartment. You have a word with Schneider. And drop in to the surgery on your way back."

***

Pete Stricker was watching a baseball game on the TV when Sheriff Johnson arrived.

The sheriff said, "I've come about the murder at the tennis club last night."

"Yes, Sheriff. A terrible business. How can I help?"

"Mort tells me you had a late night appointment with Masiak at the tennis club. Is that right?"

"Yes. He asked me to look over his tax figures."

"At two o'clock in the morning?"

"Two forty-five. He needs help … needed help, and I told him I'd be playing cards until about two. Masiak is … was a bit of a night creature anyhow, and he was single."

"And you? Are you married?"

"Divorced."

"So, did you keep the appointment?"

"Yes. I met Lance at two forty-five as arranged."

"And he gave you some figures to work on?"

"Well, no. This was our first meeting on the subject. He just outlined the general areas of concern. That was all we had planned."

"So how long was your meeting?"

"About ten minutes. I left him and went home at about three."

"And he was alive at that stage."

"Yes, Sheriff."

"You met him where, exactly?"

"In one of the squash courts. The club's general lighting is disconnected at night, but the squash courts have their own dedicated supply."

"You live alone?"

"Yes, Sheriff."

"Can anybody confirm your story?"

"George Little can, Sheriff. He came with me to the tennis club."

"Why? Did he have business with Masiak too?"

"I couldn't say, Sheriff. You'll have to ask George that."

"Was George with you when you spoke to Masiak in the squash court?"

"No, he waited outside, but he went in to speak to Masiak after I came out. Then George came out and we walked home together."

"So, do you think George killed Lance?"

"Well, Sheriff, I've been wondering about that, myself. George was quite agitated when he came out. You know. But I doubt if George could kill any one, any more than I could."

***

Mort drove out to the Schneiders' house in the suburbs. Harry fixed him a short Jack Daniels and poured one for himself.

"The sheriff asked me to call." Mort was uncomfortable with his assignment. Harry had been a good friend over the years and Mort had had a short fling with Melissa which Harry knew nothing about. "After the poker game last night, you went straight home, right?"

"Right," said Harry. "I was tired. Went straight to bed."

Melissa came in to the room with a tray of coffee and cookies. She was dressed to kill, in a tight skirt and loose blouse. She looked magnificent. All signs of her distress of that morning had been washed away in the bathtub.

She smiled at Mort conspiratorially. "So, Mort, have you made an arrest yet?"

"No, Melissa. We're not sure where to look."

"Well, I would have thought that was fairly obvious," she said.

Harry and Mort looked at one another. Harry said: "What do you mean, Sweetheart?"

Melissa smiled sweetly and said: "Oh nothing, Honey. Just kidding."

She leaned over to place the tray on the low coffee table. Mort could see her navel through the cleavage between her breasts. Then she picked up a small clutch from then tray and sat down with a satisfied look on her face.

Whistling gently, Mort said, "Harry tells me he came straight home from the game last night. The game was over at about two a.m. Right, Harry? So you would have been home by what? Two fifteen?"

"Yes. Maybe two twenty." Harry nodded.

"But Harry, it was nearly three-thirty before you came to bed," said Melissa, sweetly, crossing her legs.

"It was no later than two-twenty, Honey. You were fast asleep."

"You mean I was snoring, Darling. I was not asleep."

Harry turned bright red. He stood up and poured himself another drink. "I may have stopped off for a couple of drinks ..."

"Where?" asked Mort.

"Murphy's bar." said Harry.

"Right," said Mort. "So have either of you any idea who might have killed Lance Masiak?"

Harry said: "I hardly knew him, but he got what he deserved, I reckon."

"Harry, what do you mean?" said Melissa, her eyes wide.

"Oh, just something Pete Stricker said about him last night," Harry replied.

When the time came for Mort to leave, Melissa showed him to the door, and Mort was able to talk to her out of Harry's hearing.

"What did you mean, Melissa, when you said it was obvious who we should arrest?"

"Lance showed me the threatening letters."

"And?"

"I recognized the handwriting."

"You did?"

"Yes, definitely. Those letters were written by George."

"George Little? Are you sure?"

"Yes, of course I'm sure."

"How can you be so sure, Melissa?"

"I have some letters from George." She produced a small bundle of letters from her clutch.

Mort flicked through the top letter. "You mean you and George ..."

"Oh yes. George and I were very hot for a while. It lasted for nearly a whole summer."

"I'll have to borrow one or two of these."

"Okay, Mort, but I must have them back, and Harry mustn't know."

"Why didn't you give us this information before?"

"I was going to. Lance only showed me the threatening letters on Tuesday, after ... my squash lesson."

"I see. And you are absolutely sure about this, Melissa?"

"Oh yes, Mort. Absolutely. Why don't you ask George yourself?"

"I will." Mort whistled through his teeth. "Believe me, I will."

***

Mort made his way to the doctor's surgery. Doc Feinberg was the nearest thing they had to a forensic scientist in the town.

"Hi Doc," said Mort. "Sheriff sent me over. Have you anything for us?"

"Not much, I'm afraid, Mort. The fingernails were clean. He tried to defend himself, but his assailant was too strong for him. The rope is interesting, though."

"The rope?"

"Yes. It is an ecclesiastical accessory. Quite unusual. Much smoother than your average rope."

"What? You mean like from a monk's habit?"

"Yes. That sort of thing. Priests wear them too."

"They do?"

"Yes. They use them for ceremonial robes and Mass vestments."

***

As soon as Mort had left the Schneider house, the row started. This was a re-run of a scene that Harry and Melissa had had several times during their short married life.

Harry called Melissa a "strumpet". Melissa called Harry a "lush". Harry called Melissa a bad mother. Melissa shouted back that Harry was a poor provider. The argument never really rose above the name-calling level, and eventually Harry gave up. He found it quite difficult to get Melissa to stick to the point, and of course she admitted nothing.

Melissa went to fetch the kids from school, slamming the front door behind her.

It was early Friday afternoon, and Harry felt miserable. These scenes were a million miles from the idyllic married life which he had imagined for Melissa and himself when they both worked for the sheriff's department. He wondered whether she ever really loved him. He poured himself a small Jack Daniels.

The phone rang. It was Mike Raymer, one of Harry's poker buddies.

"Hi, Mike. Where are you?"

"Up at Lake William. Just on my way home."

"How was your trip?"

"Great. I took a small cabin in the mountains and caught some whoppers."

"Fish?" said Harry absent-mindedly.

"Yes, Harry. Of course, fish. What's the matter with you? Anyway, Harry, I rang to say I've been thinking about it, and I have decided to take that old Mustang off your hands."

"Sorry, Mike. You're too late. I sold it this morning."

Mike said, "Shit," with feeling and Harry laughed.

"Pity you didn't ring me yesterday."

"There's no phone in the cabin, or anywhere within miles of it. Shit. Shit. Shit."

"Hey, ease off on the gas, Mike. It was only a car. We do have others, you know. Come and see me when you get back to town. I'm sure I can find you something special."

"I was concerned about the money. I took the cash out of the bank today, and now I'll have to keep it with me over the weekend. I don't like carrying large amounts of cash about."

"I could lock it up in Marty's safe for you."

"Great. Thanks, Harry. I'll drop in when I get to town. I should be there by about four-thirty or five. By the way, why are you not at work? I rang Bensons but they said you were at home."

"Someone was murdered last night, in the tennis club. Melissa found the body. She was very upset, so I took the day off."

"Murdered? Are you serious? Who was it?"

"Lance Masiak, the tennis pro."

"Didn't know him. Was he a close friend?"

Harry snorted. "You could say that. A close friend of the family."

After the call, Harry knocked back his drink and poured another one.

***

On Friday afternoon, Sheriff Johnson and Deputy Mort Mooney drove round to the parish house. In the car, Mort asked the sheriff what he had found in Masiak's apartment.

"Quite an interesting set up. A false mirror and several expensive cameras, and a photographic dark room with all the gear for making your own pornography."

Mort gave a low whistle. "Any interesting photographs?"

"Lots of porn, but it was all posed, and quite soft. Oh, and this." He took a small photograph from his top pocket and handed it the Mort. It showed two naked people engaged in a sexual act. Mort recognized Pete Stricker, but not the girl. She had her back to the camera. He gave another low whistle and handed the photograph back to Sheriff Johnson.

The housekeeper opened the door and showed them into the front room. It was starting to get dark outside, but somehow it seemed darker in the room, even with the lights on. The room smelled slightly of damp. Neither of them sat down. They stood amongst the heavy furniture, peering at the dark pictures on the dark walls until Father O'Hanlon arrived.

"Sorry for keeping you, gentlemen. Please take a seat."

Mort sat down in a large chair with doubtful springs and high arms. Father Pat selected a chair under the window. Sheriff Johnson remained standing by the fireplace.

"Sorry to disturb you, Father," said the sheriff. "We are making enquiries concerning the death of Lance Masiak."

"Yes, of course. How can I help?" said Father Pat.

"I believe you were playing poker last night with Deputy Mooney and some others?"

"Yes, Sheriff. At George Little's house."

"And you left at what time?"

"I suppose it was about two o'clock."

"Where did you go after you left the game?"

"I came here, Sheriff. I came straight home."

"Did you know the victim?"

"Oh, yes, of course, Sheriff. Lance was a devout Catholic and a member of my congregation."

"What can you tell us about him, Father?"

"Not much, I'm afraid. Lance was a quiet person. He had no close family that I was aware of. His tennis was his life. I don't think he was involved in anything."

"Involved in anything?"

"I mean I don't think he was involved in anything illegal."

"What about normal pastimes?"

"Well, I really couldn't say. Perhaps you should check with some of his close friends."

"Did he have any close friends, Father?"

"Well, I don't know. He was young ... I'm sorry, Sheriff. I don't seem to be much help."

Sheriff Johnson nodded to Mort who handed Father O'Hanlon a transparent plastic bag containing the rope.

"What can you tell us about this, Father?" asked the sheriff.

Father Pat took one look at it and exclaimed, "This is amazing. Where did you find it?"

"You recognize it, Father?"

"Yes. I noticed this morning that my vestments had been tampered with and one of my ceremonial ties was missing."

"You were burgled?" Asked Mort.

"No, not burgled, exactly. The church is always open during the day, and I seldom lock the vestry door. There's nothing worth stealing in there. Some altar wine ..."

"So anyone could have walked in at any time?" said the sheriff.

"Well, yes. During daylight hours. I keep the church locked at night."

"Why didn't you report the loss?"

"Nothing else was stolen, and I have several similar ties. It seemed trivial. I thought if some poor soul had need of a piece of rope, let him have it."

"Very noble, Father, but what did you think he might have wanted it for?"

"Who knows, Sheriff? God moves in mysterious ways. Where did you find it?"

"Around Masiak's neck," replied Mort, bluntly.

Father O'Hanlon crossed himself several times. "Jesus, Mary and Joseph. You mean it was used to kill poor Lance?" He handed the plastic bag back to the sheriff.

In the car, the sheriff said to Mort "He was hiding something. I'm sure of it. I wonder what he has to lie about."

***

Deputy Mooney went home to check up on Melissa and Sheriff Johnson drove to George Little's house. The sheriff asked him if he was responsible for the anonymous letters.

He denied it, but when Sheriff Johnson produced the letters to Melissa, he broke down quickly.

He sat hunched in an armchair, tears rolling down his cheeks. Sheriff Johnson produced a large handkerchief and George blew his nose loudly.

"All right, George," said the sheriff. "What's this all about?"

"She's so vunneral, so beautiful and so vunneral, and Masiak was using her."

"You mean Melissa Schneider, George?"

George nodded.

"You must love her very much, George."

George nodded again.

"So you wrote those letters to the tennis pro, because he was using Melissa."

"Yes," said George.

"... And then, after the poker game Thursday night, you went to the tennis club and you killed him."

"No," wailed George. "I never kilt him. I sure wanted to, but, as God is my witness, I never."

"Tell us about the rope, George." said the sheriff.

"Rope?"

"Yes. The rope. Where did you get the rope, George?"

"I don't have no rope."

"Okay, George. Tell us what you did Thursday night."

"We played poker at my place. I lost. Mort was there."

"Yes, George. You played poker with Mort and the others. And after the game was over, you went out, didn't you?"

"Yes."

"Where did you go, George?"

"I went to the tennis club with Pete."

"Good. Good. You went to the tennis club with Pete, looking for Lance."

"Yes. I wanted to talk to him, to tell him to leave Melissa alone."

"So, you went to the tennis club and spoke to Lance."

"I went to the club with Pete. Pete went in and spoke to him first. Then Pete came out and I went in."

"You knew where to find him?"

"Pete told me he was in the squash court."

"Where was Pete? Did he go back in with you?"

"He waited outside."

"Ok, so you found Lance in the squash court, and then what happened?"

George wailed. "I ast him to leave Melissa alone. I told him. He shouted back at me, so I hit him."

"You hit him. With what, George?"

"I punched him. He took a swing at me, so I punched him."

"You punched him. How hard, George?"

"Pretty hard. He fell down."

"Then what happened, George?"

"I ran outside and Pete and me went home."

***

At about four o'clock, Harry went in to Bensons Autos to meet Mike Raymer. Marty was in the showroom.

"Hi Harry. Congratulations!"

"Hi Marty. Why the congratulations?"

"You off-loaded that old Mustang, finally." said Marty. He was in an unusually cheerful mood.

"Yes. An old school teacher bought it – thank God."

"And you made the twenty five percent?"

"Yes – just."

Mike Raymer arrived at five o'clock. He handed Harry a sealed brown paper parcel full of cash. Harry put it in the safe and both men went round to Murphy's bar for a drink.

"Tell me about this murder, Harry," said Mike. "Have there been any arrests?"

"I don't think so. I expect the sheriff has been talking to Pete Stricker, though."

"Why Pete?"

"Last night at the poker game, Pete said he had a late night appointment with Masiak to help him with his tax returns."

"At three o'clock in the morning? That's a bit rich, even for a tax consultant."

"Yes, we thought so."

"You said Melissa found the body."

"Yup. She was very upset. She found him sitting propped up in a corner of one of the squash courts."

At six, they left the bar. Mike gave Harry a seven pound salmon and the two men parted.

***

On Saturday morning, Pete Stricker was watching a football game on TV when Sheriff Johnson and Deputy Mort Mooney arrived. He let them in and turned off the TV sound, but left the set switched on.

"Hiya, Mort, Sheriff. Come on in. Take a seat. Can I get you something? A beer, mebbe?"

"Pete," said the sheriff. "We spoke to George Little. He confirms that you and he both went to the tennis club late on Thursday night."

"That's right, Sheriff."

"Why did you bring George with you, Pete?"

Pete grinned. "Well, I had a score to settle with Masiak, and I knew George wanted a word with him."

"You mean you knew George wanted to kill him." said the sheriff.

"No, no, Sheriff. George is big and strong ..."

"And dumb," said Mort.

"Yeah, and dumb, but he wouldn't kill anyone."

"What was this score you had to settle with Masiak?"

"Oh, nothing serious. Just gym rivalry."

Sheriff Johnson produced the photograph from Lance's apartment. He showed it to Pete and then slipped it back into his pocket.

"I think Lance was blackmailing you," said the sheriff. "I've seen the hidden cameras in his apartment."

"Okay, Sheriff. You are right," said Pete. "Lance let me use his room from time to time. I had no idea the bastard had hidden cameras. He threatened to show the photographs to my wife."

"I thought you were divorced," said Mort.

"Yeah, we are. But I've been seeing Julie again. Anyway, like I said, Lance had the photographs and I knew that George was writing those letters, so I rang Lance and arranged to meet him at the club at two forty-five."

"To pay him for the photographs?"

"Yes, Sheriff. I wouldn't want Julie to get hold of them. I have hopes that we might get back together again. You understand." Pete grinned.

"How much?" asked Mort.

"Twelve thousand."

Mort gave a long loud whistle. That was close to one year's salary for a deputy sheriff.

"So what happened? You met Lance at two forty-five, he gave you the photographs and you killed him."

"No, no, Sheriff. I met him at two forty-five, gave him the money for the photographs and left. He was alive and well at two fifty-five."

"Where are the pictures, now? Do you have them?" asked the sheriff.

"I burned them."

"And after you came out, George went in?" said Mort.

"Yeah. I saw someone else, too."

"Oh? Who?" said the sheriff.

"I saw a woman dressed in black. A tall woman. She went in after I came out, and just a few seconds after George."

"You didn't recognize her?"

"No. It was too dark. But there was something familiar about her ..."

***

Sheriff Johnson and Mort drove back to the sheriff's office in silence.

Deputy Susanne Clancy knocked and came in. "I checked out Murphy's all-night bar, Sheriff, and Harry

Schneider was there Thursday night. He left at about three o'clock."

Mort said: "So he would have had plenty of time to go to the tennis club and kill Masiak and still get home by three thirty."

"Doc Feinberg rang. He reckons Lance died between two o'clock and five o'clock." said Susanne.

"Thanks, Susanne," said the sheriff. "Please hold my calls. And maybe you could rustle up a couple of coffees."

Susanne smiled sweetly and left the room.

Sheriff Johnson said, "We now have four suspects with opportunity: Pete, Harry, George, and Father O'Hanlon. All but the priest had motive, and the weapon was Father O'Hanlon's.

Mort's head was spinning.

The sheriff said, "What did you make of Stricker's story, Mort?"

"It sounded plausible enough to me, Sheriff. He's certainly not big enough to take on Lance Masiak himself. Maybe he brought George along to do his dirty work for him."

"So why didn't he take George in with him?"

"He wanted to be sure to get the photographs from Masiak first."

"Yes, perhaps. And what about those photographs?"

"What do you mean, Sheriff?"

"Well, he is divorced, after all. Surely, he's entitled to sleep around."

"Maybe there was something else in the pictures. Something kinky?"

"Maybe. Or maybe there were no photographs at all."

"But you found one at Lance's place. The photograph in your pocket…"

"Yes. And Pete wasn't too concerned about me holding on to it."

"What about the twelve thou, Sheriff?" said Mort. "Where did that end up?"

"And who was the tall woman in black that Pete says he saw? Still lots more questions than answers, Mort."

The intercom buzzed and Susanne said: "There is a Miss Wilson here. She wants to see you, Sheriff."

"Okay," said the sheriff. He turned the blackboard to face the wall. "Wheel her in."

Miss Wilson was a grey-haired woman dressed in tweed with flat sensible shoes and a ghastly hat. Mort guessed she was in her late fifties or early sixties. She sat perched on the edge of the chair in front of the sheriff's desk, clutching her handbag. She was clearly nervous.

"Hello, Miss Wilson," said the sheriff, trying to put her at her ease. "Can I get you some coffee? Susanne, coffee for our visitor, please."

"Thank you. You are most kind," said Miss Wilson.

"Well, Miss Wilson, what can I do for you?" said the sheriff.

"I wanted to talk to you, Sheriff …"

There was a pregnant pause.

"Yes, well here I am," said the sheriff.

"Alone," said Miss Wilson, pointedly.

The sheriff shot Mort a glance and the deputy left the room.

"Right, Miss Wilson. We are alone, now. What can I do for you?"

"I am Father O'Hanlon's housekeeper."

As soon as she finished the sentence, the sheriff recognized her. He said, "Yes, Miss Wilson. We met yesterday at the parish house."

"That's right, Sheriff."

"And you have something to tell me," he prompted.

"Yes, Sheriff. It was not easy for me to come here, but I felt that you need to know about Father O'Hanlon and Lance Masiak, and I know Father O'Hanlon would never tell you himself."

She had the sheriff's complete attention, now.

There was another pause, even more pregnant than the first. Finally, she said: "I suppose you know that Father O'Hanlon served in the navy."

At that moment, Susanne came in with a coffee for Miss Wilson. Sheriff Johnson swore mentally, but he said: "Thank you, Susanne. Please see that we are not disturbed."

Susanne left and the sheriff said: "Father O'Hanlon served in the navy, you say?"

"Yes. He traveled all over the world, did all the usual sorts of things that sailors do. You understand?"

"I understand. And?"

"Well, about a year ago, Lance called to see Father O'Hanlon. He told Father O'Hanlon that he was the illegitimate son of a Polish girl living in Hamburg. His father was an American sailor."

"I see," said the sheriff. "And did the dates fit?"

"Well, apparently Father O'Hanlon was in Germany at about the right time. He became convinced that Lance was his son."

"Did they form a close friendship?"

"No, Sheriff. I think their relationship was quite strained. Then about a month ago, Lance started demanding money, and when Father O'Hanlon refused, Lance threatened to expose him to his parishioners."

"When did he make this threat?"

"A couple of weeks ago."

"Can you say what time Father O'Hanlon got in on Thursday night after the poker game?"

"No, I take sleeping pills. My health is not good. You understand."

"Yes, I understand. Thank you for coming to see me, Miss Wilson."

As soon as Miss Wilson had left, Sheriff Johnson filled Mort in on Miss Wilson's revelation.

"I think the tall woman that Pete saw at the tennis club was probably Father O'Hanlon, dressed in his cassock," he said.

"Okay," said Mort. "So where do we go from here?"

"I'm going to talk to Schneider. You go on home. I'll see you Monday morning."

***

Harry was alone in the kitchen when the sheriff called. Melissa was out at a perfume party. The kids were watching TV.

"Hi Sheriff," said Harry. "Any progress on the case?"

"Yes. Quite a bit, Harry. Do you have any beer?"

"Sure." Harry fetched a couple of beers and the two men sat at the kitchen table.

The sheriff said: "I need some help with this case, Harry, so I am going to take you into my confidence. First off, we know who wrote the threatening letters to Masiak. It was George Little. Also, George admits he met Masiak in the squash court, and he also admits that he hit him."

"So George killed him, then?"

"Possibly. He is our number one suspect at the moment. Second, we know that you left Murphy's bar at three o'clock, and that you didn't get home until three thirty, so it looks like you are our number two suspect."

Harry looked shocked. He stammered: "I … I expect I drove around for a while. I don't remember exactly. I was drinking."

"What would you say if I told you that you were seen at the tennis club?" the sheriff lied. "I think you had a bone to pick with Lance Masiak, and I think you went to the tennis club to find him."

"All right, Sheriff. I admit it. I did go round there, but I got there too late."

"What do you mean?"

"When I arrived at the tennis club, I saw Father O'Hanlon's car on the road outside. Then I saw Father O'Hanlon coming out of the club. After he was gone, I went in. I found Lance Masiak in the squash court, but he was dead. There was a nasty-looking rope around his neck. I assumed Father O'Hanlon had been giving him the last rites."

"How did you know he was dead?"

"I just knew. I left immediately and came home."

"Did you see George there? Or anyone else?"

"No, Sheriff. It never occurred to me then, but maybe Father O'Hanlon killed Masiak."

"Why would Father O'Hanlon want to kill him?"

"I have no idea."

***

The Sheriff left Harry Schneider's house, drove round to the parish house, and arrested Father O'Hanlon.

Back in the office, the sheriff confronted the priest with the evidence against him.

"In the first place, we know that Lance Masiak claimed to be your illegitimate son. You lied when you said you knew little or nothing about him. Second, we know he was trying to extort money from you. Third, Lance was murdered with a priest's ceremonial rope which you admit is yours, and fourth, you told us that you went straight home after the poker game, but you were seen at the tennis club shortly after three o'clock by two independent witnesses."

"Yes, Sheriff. I admit I did go to the tennis club on Thursday night, but I did not lie to you. I went home first and then decided to go and talk to Lance."

"To talk to Lance?"

"Yes. I wanted to convince him to give up his evil ways. I had scraped together a small amount of money and I was hoping to persuade him to leave Yuma County for good."

"And did you talk to him?"

"No, Sheriff. Sadly, I did not. I saw Pete Stricker and then George Little go in to the club and come out again. Then I went in myself, but I heard what sounded like a struggle going on in the squash courts and to my eternal shame, I took fright and left."

"What do you mean by 'a struggle?' "

"Scratching, banging sounds and heavy breathing."

"You didn't see who was involved in this struggle?"

"I saw nothing. And it grieves me that perhaps I could have saved poor Lance's life if only I had been brave enough to intervene."

"Well, if what you say is true, Father, it corroborates the stories of Stricker and Little. You didn't see Harry Schneider, did you?"

"No. Was Harry there too?"

"Yes. Harry saw you from his car. It seems almost every member of the poker school was at the tennis club early on Friday morning."

***

That night, Harry Schneider and Melissa made love. As with all truly loving couples, the process of making up after a serious argument nearly always ended in bed. Harry was his usual passionate self, but having had more than twice his usual daily ration of Jack Daniels, the process was slower than usual and Melissa was starting to enjoy herself.

There had been something nagging at the back of Harry's mind all day, although he was not even aware of it. He had a slight headache which he associated with the whiskey, but which was actually caused by the sluggish grinding of the cogs of his subconscious mind, working away in first gear.

Unfortunately, the revelation hit him at a moment when all of his attention should have been on the task in hand.

"Oh my God!" he exclaimed, and rolled away from Melissa onto his back.

"What's the matter, Harry?" enquired Melissa. "Are you ill?"

"No. Not ill. Dumb. I think I know who killed Lance. I'll have to ring the sheriff."

He climbed out of bed and pulled on some clothes.

Melissa was not pleased. "Harry, please come back to bed. It's the middle of the night. Please, Harry. You can ring him in the morning."

But Harry was gone. He took the stairs two at a time, went into the kitchen and rang Sheriff Johnson at home.

"Sheriff?"

"Yes. Who's that?"

"Harry. Harry Schneider."

"Harry? What time is it?"

"I don't know. Sheriff, listen. I think I know who killed Lance."

"Harry. It's two o'clock in the morning. Can't it wait until the morning?"

"Yes. I suppose so."

"Great, so I can go back to sleep, can I?"

"Yes," said Harry, "but don't you want to know who killed Lance?"

"All right. Tell me. Who was it?"

"It was Mike. Mike Raymer"

"Great, Harry. Thanks for the information. Come to the office in the morning and we'll talk about it. Now, goodnight."

***

Harry was waiting for the sheriff when he arrived at his office the next morning.

The Sheriff opened the office and they just made it inside before Harry started to explain his theory.

"It came to me last night."

"Yes, I sort of gathered that."

"Mike rang me on Friday afternoon, from somewhere up country."

"He was on one of his fishing trips?"

"Yes. He rang me from Lake William. Then he drove straight to Bensons. He wanted me to lock up the money in Benson's safe."

"Money? What money?"

"Mike said he wanted to buy the Mustang. He said he had the money with him."

"You are losing me, Harry. What Mustang?"

"Right," said Harry. "I bought a 1965 Mustang from a hippie, about six months ago. Mike said he wanted to buy the car."

"So you sold it to him?"

"No. I sold it to a retired schoolmarm."

"A retired teacher. Do I know her?"

"No. Maybe. I don't know. That's not important."

"Right, so Mike wanted to buy this Mustang? But you had sold it to someone else."

"Yes. Mike said that he had already taken the cash out of the bank, so he asked me to put it in the safe for the weekend."

"Okay. And what else?"

"I had a drink with Mike after we put the money in the safe. I told him about Pete's meeting with Lance, and he said three o'clock was a bit late even for a tax consultant."

                    JJ TONER

"Yes?"

"How did he know the time of the meeting? I didn't tell him."

"Well, maybe it was a lucky guess. He was fifteen minutes out. Maybe he spoke to one of the other poker players before he spoke to you."

"No. He couldn't have. He drove straight from Lake William to Bensons."

"Right. So he drove straight from the cabin at Lake William to Bensons to put the money in the safe? It's a bit thin, isn't it, Harry? What's Mike's motive for murder?"

"I don't know, Sheriff."

The sheriff thought for a moment. Then he said, "Ring Marty Benson. Ask him to meet us at the car lot."

"But it's Sunday, Sheriff."

"Yes, I know, but I want to take a look at the money you put in the safe."

"Why? What do you expect to find?"

"Twelve thousand dollars."

***

The sheriff rang Mike Raymer. "Meet me at Bensons Autos. I need your opinion about something."

This sort of request was not unusual. Mike was a youth leader and the young people in his care often ran foul of the law, so Mike was quite used to calls from the sheriff.

"Yeah, sure, Sheriff. Give me twenty minutes."

When Mike arrived at the car lot, he found Marty Benson, Harry Schneider and the sheriff waiting in Marty's office.

"Hi, Harry. Marty. Hi, Sheriff," said Mike. "What's up?"

"Hi Mike," said the sheriff. "Well for starters, you can tell me why you murdered Lance Masiak."

Mike grinned. "What? You're kidding, of course, Sheriff."

"No joke, Mike. I know you did it. I just want to know why."

"But you know I've been away on a fishing trip ..."

"Yes. I know that. But you came back to town on Thursday night, stole a rope from the vestry and murdered Lance in the tennis club."

"Come on, Sheriff. You can't be serious. Do I look strong enough to strangle a tennis pro?"

"The victim had been knocked unconscious before you got to him."

"Who by?"

"By George Little. Also, I think Pete Stricker was in it with you. He lured Masiak to the tennis club that night."

"So why would Pete and me want to kill this tennis pro?"

"Pete told us about the photographs."

"But he burned them."

"So you knew about the photographs."

"Yes. Pete and I are friends. He tells me things. Look here, Sheriff. This is all nonsense. What proof do you have?"

Sheriff Johnson nodded to Harry.

"Well Mike," said Harry. "Remember you rang me about the Mustang?"

"On Friday. Yes."

"You told me that you had taken the money out of the bank to pay for the car."

"That's right."

"And that money is in this safe."

"Yes. You put it there on Friday."

"Right, Marty. Open it up and let's take a look," said the sheriff. Marty spun the dial on the safe. The sheriff continued: "I think we will find twelve thousand dollars in the safe. I think you stole Pete Stricker's money from Lance Masiak when you strangled him."

Mike sat on the edge of Marty's desk with his arms crossed. He said nothing.

The safe swung open. Marty took out the brown paper parcel. It was still sealed. Harry opened it and counted the money.

"Six thousand, four hundred and fifty dollars," he said.

"What was the price on the Mustang?" said Mike, triumphantly.

"Six thousand, four hundred and fifty dollars," Harry replied.

"Exactly right," snorted Mike. "Can I go now?"

"But Mike," said Harry, "I marked the car price down on Thursday. Before Thursday, the price was seven thousand dollars. It was seven thousand for months."Mike turned white, suddenly.

"So you must have been in town on Thursday."

"I rang Pete on Friday, before I spoke to you. He told me what the new price was."

"And then you went to the bank before ringing me?"

"Yes ..."

"That won't wash either, Mike. Pete was with me when I sold the car. He would have told you that it was gone."

"Well I must have rung Pete on Thursday, so."

"From the cabin?"

"Yes."

"But you told me there was no phone in the cabin, or anywhere near it. Remember?"

Suddenly, it was all over. Mike broke down and confessed.

Father O'Hanlon was released. Pete was arrested. Once in the jail, both men began hurling accusations at one another and the whole story came out.

***

"But why were Mike and Pete working together?" asked Melissa.

Harry smiled his Sherlock Holmes smile. He said: "Pete and Mike were lovers. The photographs were explicit pictures of Pete and Mike. There was no girl involved. Mike's position as a youth leader made him particularly vulnerable to a blackmailer."

"Wow!" said Melissa. "Pete! And Mike Raymer!" She shuddered. "Poor Julie! What happened to the money?"

"Mike recovered the money after killing Lance and returned it to Pete."

"Why did they involve poor George?"

"Elementary, my dear Melissa. They involved George in the hope that he might have killed Lance, and when he left Lance alive, they reverted to 'Plan B' and finished him off themselves. George was Pete's alibi. Mike's fishing trip was his."

"So why did they use Father O'Hanlon's rope?"

"Plan B involved framing Father Pat for the murder, because they knew that Lance had been trying to extort money from him, so he had a motive, and also, Mike and Pete probably suspected that Father O'Hanlon knew about their illicit relationship and was going to blow the whistle on them."

"And you worked all this out yourself?"

"Well, the sheriff helped a bit."

"You are clever, Harry. Let's go upstairs."

TATTOOIST

First published by JJ Toner Publishing, 2015

One damp day in mid-September 1968, judging that the season was over, I hauled the boat out onto the slipway at Dunquin, intending to return the next day to secure it for the winter. I stopped off in Crean's for a pint on my way home.

There was a stranger at the bar who offered to buy me a pint.

He seemed pleasant enough. He had a high forehead with a receding hairline and a large angular nose which stood out from his face like the Matterhorn. I guessed he was in his early thirties. He was dressed in tweeds and sturdy walking boots.

"My name's Grant. Peter Grant. I'm from London," he said, sipping the head off his pint. I sank half of mine in one gulp.

"Sean Whelan. On holiday, are you?"

"Yes. I'm here to do some fishing."

I told him a little about myself and he said he was a writer.

"What sort of things do you write about?"

"True Crime, criminals. That sort of thing."

"You won't find too many of them around here," I said.

He laughed. "I told you, I'm here for the fishing. Perhaps you could help me find a boat."

"I can do better than that," I said. "Meet me at Dunquin harbour tomorrow morning at nine and I'll take you out."

***

The next day was sunny, but with a fresh breeze. I took Pop's old Morris Minor into Dunquin. It was close to ten by the time I stepped from the car.

Grant was waiting for me on the slipway. We lowered the boat into the water and the engine into the boat. Once the engine was attached and fuelled, I helped the Englishman into the boat, handed him down two rods, and cast off. Pointing the boat at the Great Blasket Island, I opened the throttle.

Turning left, I set us on a course parallel to the shore. About half way across the Sound, level with Beiginis, I cut the engine and we dropped our feathered lines in the water. After about three minutes, we hit the mackerel. The beggars couldn't get enough of our feathers and we caught a boatful.

We had a few pints in Moriarty's, and I invited Grant back to the cottage where Mam fried a couple of mackerel and a feed of chips. After the meal he peered at the few photographs that we had on the walls. I showed him some of Pop's designs and told Grant his story.

Pop was born in Poland in 1915, and was interned by the Nazis in the concentration camp at *Majdanek* in 1940. After the war he moved to Ireland and was resettled in our cottage near Annascaul. He changed his name to Mick

Whelan, and rented the small shop in Dingle. He never spoke about his time at the camp and we knew never to ask.

Pop was my world. In my early teens my life had turned into a nightmare through bullying and the attentions of a deviant priest. In defiance of the education authorities, Pop had solved all my problems by taking me out of school at fifteen. He bought me the boat and the outboard motor and taught me how to use them. Everything I knew about fishing the Sound I'd learnt from him. The priest was re-located to another parish.

Grant told us about his own life in London; how, after five years as a successful stockbroker, he had quit his job to try and make it as a writer. Brought up in an orphanage, everything he achieved was through his own hard work. I admired his stubborn approach to life which was so like Pop's.

We waited until it started to get dark, then I took him back to his lodgings in Mrs Moynihan's B&B.

"Pity you missed Pop," I said. "You would like him."

"Damn shame," he replied with feeling.

It was three days before I saw Grant again. He was sitting alone in a dark corner of Crean's early in the afternoon, nursing a whiskey. He'd had a few. I sat down at the table opposite him.

"Where've you been hiding, Sean? I haven't seen you lately."

"I've been busy. Shouldn't you be back in London yourself by now?"

"I still have work to finish here." He waved his cigarette in my face.

"Work? I thought you were on holiday."

"It's a sort of working holiday."

"What kind of work?"

"Research. Family matters." He tapped the side of his nose.

"Your family has Irish connections?"

"Not Irish. Polish."

"You're joking!"

"No joke, Sean."

He ordered a refill for me and a Paddy's for himself.

After a long silence, he said, "Peter Grant's not my real name."

"What is it, then?"

"Walenski. Pavel Walenski."

I laughed, "Walenski is Pop's name."

"I know." He poked a finger in my chest. "I've been searching for your father for twelve years."

"For Pop?"

"My father was taken to a concentration camp when I was just three years old. I haven't seen him since. I've spent the last twelve years on his trail."

"And it led you here?"

"Eventually. It hasn't been easy."

"What's your father's full name?"

"Michal Walenski."

I was gob-smacked. "Still, there must be lots of Michal Walenskis in Poland," I said. "How can you be sure he's the right one?"

He took out a small pocket book and turned to a page with a seven-digit number written on it. He copied the number onto a beer mat and handed it to me.

I stared at it blankly. "What's this?" Before he could answer I realised exactly what it was. Pop carried a number tattooed on his left inner arm – the legacy of his time spent in the concentration camp. Growing up, I must have seen the number on Pop's arm a thousand times, and yet I couldn't recall it. To me, it was just a symbol, not really a number at all.

"I got it from the records at Lubin," he said. "God knows why, but the Nazis kept records. Name, age, sex, number."

"So, if this is the number on Pop's arm, then he must be your father?"

He knocked back his drink and said, "And we would be half-brothers!"

I never had a brother, or even a half-brother. The idea gave me goose bumps and sent a tingle up my spine. Mam had no recollection of Pop ever having mentioned a son, but she often said he was so secretive about his former life that nothing would surprise her.

***

The next day, Pop and I went out to the bog to lay out some turf for the winter. Pop was a small man, older than his years but physically strong, bald on top and with thick blue veins standing out on the backs of his large hands. It was a warm, overcast day and we were soon stripped to the waist, Pop working the ancient fibres from the ground and throwing them out to me to place in small stacks for drying. It wasn't difficult to check the number on his left arm and compare it with the number on the beer mat.

They were identical.

In the evening, before we drove home, I broke the good news to him. As my story unfolded, his eyes lit up and his huge fists clenched. I knew that look. It was no surprise when he hit me. As I lay sprawled on the ground nursing my jaw, he stood over me.

"You had no business talking about me to strangers!" he roared. "How many times must I tell you: my past is dead and forgotten?"

"What d'you want me to do, Pop?" I said. "I could tell him the numbers don't match."

"No, the ship's out of the bottle now. No way you can put it back. Tell him I'll meet with him here. Tonight. Alone."

"What time?"

"After dark."

***

That night, the storm broke. Like the tongues of giant reptiles, sheet after sheet of lightning flashed and shimmered across the bay. To the west, thunder clouds had built up over the Blaskets and the rain pounded down on Mount Eagle. It was as if the Gods had finally decided to wash the ancient mountain into the sea.

Close to midnight, Pop entered the cottage. He stood by the door and gestured to me. I put on my coat and followed him out into the night. The thunder had rolled on to the north-west through Conor Pass, and lightning flashed over Mount Brandon.

I followed Pop up to the road and opened the passenger door of the car. The Englishman was sitting crouched in the back seat, a large rucksack beside him. His face was deathly white. His eyes were open. There was a deep gash on the side of his head. The wound had stopped bleeding but his tweed collar was saturated with blood.

"Pop?" was all I managed to say. My hands were shaking.

"He's dead," Pop said. "We have to get rid of the body."

We.

"You killed him?"

"We'll talk about it later."

I grabbed Pop by the shoulders and shook him.

"Tell me now," I screamed. "Tell me why you killed him."

From the wild look in his eyes, I thought he might hit me again, but he didn't. He shook free of my grip. "I had to, Sean." He walked around the car and climbed in behind the wheel. I opened the passenger door, and hesitated.

"Get in," he shouted.

I got in and slammed the door. I had little choice. I hated what he'd done, but he was my father, and he needed my help.

The car moved forward, rear wheels spinning on the softening road surface, windscreen wipers struggling with the deluge. We drove in silence until we reached the harbour.

"He was your son, Pop," I said. "He was my *brother*."

He shook his head, peering straight ahead through the windscreen. "He was no son of mine."

The small harbour was deserted. Pop slung the rucksack over one shoulder. Then he pulled Grant from the car and dragged him down the slipway. "Bring the engine," he shouted above the wind.

I lifted the outboard motor from the boot of the car, carried it down the slipway, and attached it to the back of the boat.

"Help me," he said.

The storm clouds were directly overhead, now, the driving rain running over my bare head and down my face.

"I can't." I stared at him. This was where Pop would come to my rescue again, explain everything with a word and make the whole problem disappear with a wave of his hand.

He straightened his back and looked at me for a long moment, Grant's upper body resting against Pop's lower legs. "We have to get him into the boat. Help me, son," was all he said.

I knew what he was going to do. Grant's body would be dumped in the Sound, food for the mackerel.

"I want no part of this!" I shouted. "You killed him. It's nothing to do with me." I took a step backwards.

"You're already involved," he shouted back. "Just help me get him into the boat."

He was right, of course. I was already an accessory. I took hold of Grant's legs, and we lifted him into the boat.

"Wait for me here." He started the engine and set off across the Sound. I stood and watched the boat until it disappeared in the darkness, knowing that I would never fish these waters again.

***

As we drove home, the clouds parted and there was a moon. The landscape looked unnatural in the strange light, like a hollow promise.

I said, "Why did you have to kill him?"

"Why d'you think?"

I took a deep breath. "I think you stole his father's identity at the end of the war."

He said nothing, staring ahead at the road.

I continued, "You tattooed his number on your own arm."

I stopped there and waited for him to say something. After a few moments he said, "Anything else?" and I knew I was on the right track.

"Were you at that concentration camp at all?"

"I was at the camp."

"But you weren't a prisoner."

No response.

"What were you? A guard?"

"I was the camp tattooist. Go on."

I closed my eyes and the delicate Celtic designs in the window of Pop's tattoo parlour appeared like after-images on the inside of my eyelids.

"Are you even Polish?" I dreaded the answer to this question.

"Yes, I was Polish. I'm Irish now. I barely escaped. All I had was Walenski's papers and his number. Without those, I would never have made it out of Poland alive."

I thought about what it must have been like at the end of the war; the Russians advancing, the German army in full flight; the workers in the camp rising up, exacting gruesome revenge on the guards and on the Poles who collaborated with them. If they had got their hands on Pop he would have been torn apart.

We drove back to the cottage in silence.

He pulled in beside the cottage and switched off the engine. "What happened to the real Michal Walenski?" I said, dreading the answer.

"He died. A lot of people died then."

I took another deep breath and said, "How did he die? Did you kill him?"

He looked at me and our eyes locked. "You can't believe that. I'm no killer."

"You killed Grant!"

"I told you. I had to." The look in his eyes said: Leave it!

But I had to ask. "Why? You still haven't told me why."

Pop averted his eyes. "He worked out what happened. He worked out who I was and what I'd done. He would have gone back to London and exposed me. That would have been the end of me – of all of us. What else could I do?"

Before we went inside, he said, "You must say nothing of this to anyone, Sean."

"Mam?"

"No one. With any luck Grant will be forgotten and that'll be the end of it."

"He may have family in London," I said, praying that it was true.

"He had no one. He was a struggling writer. He had no ties. He told me."

"Friends, neighbours, a girlfriend?" Surely he couldn't just disappear without anybody noticing.

"We'll just have to hope nobody cares enough to sound the alarm," he said.

We again. We were in this together.

I said, "Mrs Moynihan will miss him."

He shook his head. "He'd left his lodgings, paid the bill."

I thought about this. Nothing ever gets past Mrs Moynihan. "Even so, she's a danger." I was sounding more and more like a co-conspirator.

"Don't worry about it. Leave Mrs Moynihan to me."

I glanced at him, but his face was expressionless. Was he going to feed the old lady to the fishes too?

We got out of the car and he stood very close to me. His hands were fists again. "Just remember: you are an accessory. If I go to jail, so will you. Think what that would do to Mam."

I nodded.

He took three seconds to consider his next words. "We're safe enough, son. Even if someone raises the alarm, there's no physical evidence."

***

Two days passed. Pop hung around the house, but I avoided him as much as I could. The cottage was unnaturally quiet, and it seemed darker than usual, like the inside of a coffin. Images of Grant's body rolling in the current of the Sound filled my mind. I could see the mackerel plucking at his tweed coat and then at his flesh, his hands, his face.

Every moment that passed I expected a loud knock on the door, but none came. Perhaps Pop was right. Perhaps Grant would never be missed and he would just cease to be, the memory of his existence fading from anyone who ever knew him.

Early on the third day I put my coat on and took the car keys from the mantelpiece.

"Where're you off to?" Mam said.

"I have to lay the boat down for the winter."

Pop said, "I'll come with you, son," putting his newspaper aside.

"I want to do this one my own, Pop," I replied.

He hesitated. Then he shrugged and returned to his paper.

***

Foot to the floor, I drove to the harbour under a darkening sky. The outboard motor was still in the car boot. I pulled it out, lugged it down the slipway, and attached it to the boat. I started the engine, opened the throttle and headed out across the Sound.

If I followed the current there was just a chance that I might find Grant's body, or his rucksack.

The boat became the plaything of the wind-frenzied sea, lifting and slapping, lifting and slapping through the waves, while above me, a lone seagull battled against the storm.

As I cleared the lee of the islands, the full force of the gale hit, tossing the small boat about like a cork. The current through the Sound was as strong as I had ever known it. I mouthed a prayer, clinging to the side of the bucking boat.

That was when I spotted it – a small black rectangle at my feet. Grant's notebook. I picked it up and tucked it away inside my coat.

I turned the boat and headed back towards the shore.

As the engine laboured against the elements, I shouted out every profanity I knew. I had the evidence I needed to go to the police. I screamed. Only the gull heard me. I wept, and the rain and the sea spray washed away my tears.

JUSTIFIABLE HOMICIDE

IT NEVER RAINS BUT it pours. What smart alec came up with that? Whoever he was, he knew his onions.

We had just sold our house. We put our furniture in storage and moved in to her mother's for a few weeks while the new place was being finished.

Well, actually it was finished, but I decided to delay payment of the balance of the money for a while, to make the builder sweat. That way, I could get him to put in a few extras, improve the overall finish of the house, add some extra lighting fixtures, and do a bit of landscaping in the garden – that sort of thing.

We were sitting pretty. With our house sold we had cash in the bank gaining interest. And living rent-free with the mother-in-law, I was in no great hurry to complete. Melanie was a bit fidgety, of course. She was itching to get in and measure the windows for curtains.

So far so good, you might say, and I suppose I would have gone on to live a full and uneventful life if I hadn't lost my job just at that time. It's amazing how easily and how quickly things can change. Within twenty-four hours, I went from middle-income pillar of the community to homeless free-loader with no prospects. Two months after that, I was near-destitute and universally hated.

I'm hoping for an all-male jury, by the way. If there are no women, I'd be confident of a verdict of justifiable homicide, or manslaughter at worst.

***

I worked in the Accounts department at Pillwell Engineering, where I had applied for a more senior job, newly created. I thought the interview had gone quite well. Then one day about three weeks after the interview I was called in to Martin Dimmock's office on the sixth floor, to be handed my promotion – or so I thought. I sat down opposite the director with a big, silly smile on my face.

"As you know," Dimmock said. "We have been conducting interviews for the new post of Senior Administration Coordinator in the Accounts Section."

I nodded. My smile broadened.

"Well the interview process has been completed now ..." He paused in mid-sentence and used the tip of his finger to push his spectacles up his nose.

That simple gesture told me what was coming next. My heart tumbled into the pit of my stomach, the smile froze on my big, silly face.

He rumbled on. "... Not incognizant of your undoubted talents ... on balance ... the best all round candidate ... We are sure you will work well with Maria Lawless."

Maria Lawless! If they had given the job to someone of equal status to myself – Daniels in Accounts Payable, or even Blaylock in Shipping, then I could have lived with it – grudgingly, perhaps. But Maria Lawless was from the

junior ranks, and that immediately made my position un-
tenable.

In a flash I realised that the whole thing, the new job, the
interviews – everything – was just a huge conspiracy to get
rid of me. The whole board of directors must have been
in on it, and their plan had worked perfectly. Like a fool, I
had swallowed the whole thing, hook, line and sinker.

I resigned immediately, of course. Dimmock never
blinked. He said how sorry they were to lose me and asked
me to hand over the keys to the company car. He stood
up and accompanied me to the boardroom door, where he
shook my hand and wished me well in my future career.

I stormed from the office and went for a long walk. I
needed to get right away from everybody I knew in there,
to avoid their knowing glances. And I needed to think – to
take stock of my situation.

My mind was in turmoil. To start with all I could think
of was how much time I had invested in the company – I
had been with them for nearly fifteen years – and how sudden, how brutal the separation. How could the company
function without me? Could it? Surely not. Obviously,
the directors thought it could, while in reality, without
me the whole edifice would come crashing down around
them.

Sooner or later.

Serve them right!

With that thought I began to feel a little better. Like a
sailor in a lifeboat cut adrift by the mutinous crew of a
doomed ship. I laughed. Perhaps I was the lucky one; the
rest of them would go down with the ship.

I'd give them a year, two max.

I was forty-two and healthy. I was well on the way toward giving up the cigarettes and I had quite firm plans to get more exercise and lose some weight. So what were my chances of getting another job? I tried to be optimistic, seeking out my strong points, my qualifications, my extensive experience. But panic began to set in – slowly at first, like a tingling sensation around the base of the skull, and then washing over me like a cold shower. I was over the hill, overweight and probably unemployable. No matter how I reasoned, no matter which way I turned, I could not escape the stark reality of the dole queue.

Clearly, the house purchase would have to be cancelled. Thank God I had delayed the deal, or I would have been in real trouble, with a new mortgage on top of everything else. I rang my solicitor and explained the situation to him. He said he was sorry to hear the bad news and went off to see if he could recover my deposit from the builder.

Some people have no conscience! The builder refused to refund my deposit, and the solicitor took his fees from the portion of the money which he held. The carpet shop also refused to refund my deposit. So much for friendship and sympathy for your fellow man! I suppose they remembered the unpleasantness over that faulty hall stairs and landing carpet in our first house. I did no more than stand up for my rights as a consumer, and I expect they offloaded their shoddy merchandise on some other unsuspecting guy. But there had been some harsh words exchanged and they obviously held a grudge.

I got back to the mother-in-law's house earlier than usual that day.

Melanie said, "How was work, Dan?"

"Fine," says I.

She said, "Where's the car?" and I told her it was gone for a service. Her mother gave me a funny look, but she said nothing.

The next day was Saturday and Melanie wanted to go shopping for clothes as usual, so she had to take a taxi. The thought of all that money in the bank must have gone to her head, because she over-indulged herself even more than usual, running up a credit card bill of gargantuan proportions.

***

On Monday morning, I went to the local job centre and registered. I was interviewed by a spotty youth of about twenty-five who had no idea about Accounts Administration and hadn't a clue what questions to ask. I'm afraid I lost my rag and used a few well-rounded expletives. I thumped his desk and told him to stuff his psychometric tests where the sun don't shine. He was visibly alarmed at my assertive attitude.

I got back to the house at lunch time. Melanie was surprised to see me, but suspected nothing. Melanie's mother immediately picked up the scent of trouble. It's funny how mothers-in-law seem to have an infallible instinct for a weak spot. She squinted at me with a toad eye and said, "You're home very early. You haven't lost your job, have you?"

I managed to laugh that off, but it was a narrow squeak, and I don't think the old witch was completely convinced.

Anyway, from then on I stayed out of the house until about six, which is when I would have got home if I still had the job. Most days, I took the bus to various distant parts of the city and went for long walks. I convinced Melanie that the car had to be sent away to have new maneuvering thrusters fitted. Melanie's mother was not pleased. She demanded to know how she was supposed to get to her flower arranging classes on Wednesday nights. I told her she had a perfectly good broomstick. As for the new house, I had to be quite inventive about the various serious faults which had only now become apparent. We couldn't think about moving in until they were all fixed. Standards of workmanship are so poor nowadays.

After a week, Melanie asked, "How's the car coming, Dan? Have they replaced those whatcha-me-call-ems?"

"The plasma flow inducers. No. They had to send to the factory for some new ones, and there's likely to be a delay."

"How long?"

"A week or two, I expect," I said.

***

After a month, I broke the news to Melanie that the new house had subsided and there was now no way that we could buy it. She wanted to go round to take a look, but I explained that the whole area had been cordoned off by the construction police as it was a serious health hazard. Melanie's mother was very upset, of course. She wanted to know when we were planning to move out. She complained about my smoking and about Melanie's untidiness and of course she had to bring the Rottweilers into it. She never liked our dogs, even when they were living in our house, but since they moved to her house she had become unreasonable about them. I mean, it's only natural for dogs to bark at cats. That's what dogs do. And she had only herself to blame about the mess. I expect she traumatized the poor animals by her obvious hostility towards them. They were perfectly well house-trained in our house.

The car, of course, was never repaired. The official story was that the faulty anti-matter injectors were replaced okay, but then there was a nasty warp core breach, and that was that.

***

Three weeks ago, Melanie's mother bumped into my solicitor's secretary in the supermarket, and the cat was out of the bag. Melanie was furious when she realized that for the past six months we had been living on our capital. There wasn't a lot of it left, and we had built up quite a hefty credit card bill.

Mother-in-law's cat had taken to staying out a lot, just dropping in from time to time for its meals. Finally, last week it disappeared altogether and Melanie's mother went ballistic. She directed all of her anger at me, for some reason. Melanie can do no wrong, of course. She said Melanie should never have married me in the first place. She said I was invading her "space" and she wanted it back. Then Melanie joined in. She kept asking me where we were going to live and what we were supposed to live on. I didn't have answers to any of her questions, so I took the dogs for a long walk to get away from the two women and have a good think.

We went down to the woods and I let the dogs off their leads for a bit. It occurred to me quite out of the blue, that Melanie's mother was the real problem. If she lived somewhere else, her house was quite big enough for Melanie and me and the dogs. It was Melanie's mother who was taking up too much space. And most of the rows and unpleasantness were her fault. Then I was struck by an inspired thought. What if she died suddenly? Nobody would notice. Melanie would inherit the house and her mother's investments and we would be very comfortable.

Before returning to the house, I filled my pockets with toadstools, concentrating on the most colorful ones I could find.

***

As luck would have it both women were planning to watch The X-Factor, so I offered to cook the evening meal. Mushroom omelette for mother-in-law, and, since Melanie is allergic to eggs, toasted sandwiches for Melanie and me. It was perfect, I thought, she'll never suspect a thing.

How wrong can you be? She took one sniff of her omelette, gave me a withering look, and put the plate on the floor. Before you could say Jack Russell, the Rottweilers had scoffed the lot.

The dogs were a dead weight, the vet sympathetic. There was nothing he could do. He reckoned it must have been something they ate. Dogs are notoriously voracious eaters and often die of accidental poisoning. He showed me some published statistics on the subject. Greater than twenty-five percent of dogs die this way. Who knew?

Melanie's mother stopped talking to me altogether after that, and I thought I detected a creeping iciness in Melanie's attitude, too.

I left the house and headed for the pub to come up with a revised plan. The talk in the pub was all about recent burglaries in the neighborhood. People had been surprised in their beds by intruders; casual violence had been experienced. Maybe, thought I, if I left a window open at the front of the house, we might be burgled. The old dear's heart couldn't be too strong at her age; coming face to face with a burglar in her bedroom might just finish her off. And that was when I formulated plan B.

Like all the best plans, it was simplicity itself.

First, I planted the seed. I told Melanie about the burglaries. She was horrified, of course, and took to sleeping with my seven iron beside her bed. Then I waited a few days before swinging into action.

I chose a moonless night. At three o'clock, when everyone was tucked up in bed, I dressed in my darkest clothes and left the house.

I broke in through the kitchen window.

The house was quiet as the morgue.

Slipping into the living room, I opened the bookcase and scattered the contents on the floor. Then I emptied every drawer I could find. I surveyed my work. It was impressive. Clearly the work of a hardened criminal.

I snuck up the stairs and into the mother-in-law's bedroom. Her ladyship lay on her back, her mouth agape. I picked up a spare pillow and approached the bed. The old woman lay very still. She wasn't snoring. She wasn't moving. She didn't even seem to be breathing. I checked her pulse. No pulse, and she was cold.

Dead as the bedpost.

My first reaction was one of relief, as you can imagine. Nature had taken its course and done the deed for me. My second reaction was joy. My troubles were over. Melanie would inherit the house and the old dear's investments and we'd be in clover for the rest of our lives. I gave a whoop, a jig and a waltz with the pillow as dancing partner.

Melanie's scream took me completely by surprise. Before I could say anything, she hit me with the seven iron. A glancing blow, but enough to knock me off my feet. She took a second swing which I managed to evade by rolling out of the way. I jumped up and we wrestled with the club.

"It's me," I said. No effect.

I shouted, "Melanie, it's Dan." Still no joy. She carried on tugging at the club.

It was dark, but even so, I thought she must have known it was me under the balaclava.

***

When I pushed her against the banister railing, the railing broke. The fall broke her neck. They found me in the hall cradling her head. I suppose I might have concocted a story if I'd changed into my pajamas and hidden the balaclava. And I probably would have if the police hadn't arrived so quickly. Melanie must have rung them before tackling me in her mother's bedroom.

So what do you think? Self-defense, an accident, manslaughter or justifiable homicide?

JUDGMENT DAY

Saint Peter is waiting at the gates of heaven. He keeps checking his watch. There's no getting away from it: the end is nigh and getting nigher with every passing moment. From his vantage point he can see and all the people rushing about below like headless chickens. Billions of them. The only large animals that still outnumber the human race are the rats.

He and Gabriel had booked a holiday for the second half of the twenty-first century. He's going to have to cancel that. As soon as the proverbial brown stuff hits the whirly thing, he is going to be busy. And that is bound to happen any year now.

God Almighty is probably laughing up His sleeve. Nobody knows exactly, on account of His eternal veil, but loud chuckling thunder has been heard coming from His throne room, and young Lucifer has a permanent smug grin on his face, having placed a massive CFD short trade on the outcome of the human experiment sometime during the early Jurassic.

The switch from farming to ranching might have been sustainable – if a tad inconsiderate to the animals – if the human population had remained at reasonable levels. And God knows He did His best to keep the dampers on it with lots of famines, plagues and the occasional world war. But from the moment that Stephenson chap invented his first steam engine, the writing was on the wall. The discovery of black gold and the invention of the internal combustion engine didn't help, and when Henry Ford started producing motor cars for the masses, the whole process began to accelerate like a runaway train. Next came the building of huge electricity generating stations fuelled by coal and oil, and the destruction of the forests to create – you've guessed it – more land for farming to support the ever-burgeoning population.

Talk about a vicious circle!

Their pathetic attempts to recover the situation were painful to watch. A feeble Climate Accord set up at the eleventh hour and then abandoned by the president of one of the worst offenders, protests by schoolchildren, and lots of pie-in-the sky plans: electric cars, solar energy, wind energy, wave energy, nuclear power plants, carbon taxes and the final craziness: a rocket to take rich folks to Mars.

The only question remaining is who to blame. It's not called Judgment Day for nothing. Someone has to sit in judgment and someone has to take the blame. I'm calling this meeting to order.

We can't blame historical figures like Robert Stephenson or Robert Street, the Wright brothers or Wernher von Braun; they thought they were contributing towards 'progress', and they were. The problem was that all this progress was leading, like a runaway train, to a man-made mass extinction event.

Without further ado, I propose that we turn the spotlight of blame on He who conceived the whole experiment in the first place. You could argue that He really should have foreseen the final outcome. Omniscience has its own inherent obligations, after all.

His first mistake was to give them curiosity. That led to Science and the 'scientific method'. Think how much better off the world would be if it had been left in the hands of the shamans, the religious zealots, the magicians, the sorcerers, the alchemists, and the astrologists. No atomic weapons, for a start. No weapons of any kind, peace and enlightenment all round, with the Leos in charge.

His second mistake was giving them intelligence. Those big brains gave them ideas way beyond their station and fuelled their insatiable curiosity. There's nothing worse than a know-it-all ape with attitude and an ego to go with it.

His third mistake was those opposable thumbs. Think how little 'progress' they would have made if all they had was horses' hooves or dolphin flippers.

His fourth mistake was teaching them to talk. The tower of Babel was a pretty ineffective attempt to set that to rights. Of course giving them lots of languages so that they could only communicate within their own tribes led to conflict at first. Inevitably, this stumbling block to progress was overcome.

His fifth mistake was making the males physically stronger than the females. All that testosterone was bound to cause problems. A world dominated by women probably would have gone the same way in the long run, but there would have been a lot more fun, great art and music sloshing around in the world before the end.

His worst mistake was giving them Free Will. Michael and the rest of us tried to warn Him against that, but would He listen? Does He ever? Michael has been heard to say that the Garden of Eden event was the greatest deal breaker. Edengate, he calls it. Perhaps we should concede the point now, in hindsight, the only thing more tempting than temptation is temptation in the hands of a woman.

With hindsight, ecology was a bad joke; nothing but a spiralling food chain, perched precariously on the capricious whims of unregulated evolution. How on earth could that have worked? As long as the whole system was in balance it was fine, but the slightest upset, like the loss of a link in the chain, was bound to bring the whole edifice crashing down like a house of cards.

So, no need for a judge or jury. I think we are all agreed. The guilty party is clearly identified by His deeds, ill-conceived, badly managed and poorly executed, starting with that ridiculous Big Bang!

All in favour of a guilty verdict raise your tentacles.

OF ELEPHANTS AND DWARVES

The body lay on the carpet in a pool of blood.

"Disturb nothing," Soames said in his practiced tone of authority. With his customary stoop, he stood quite still, his tall, imposing frame resplendent in his greatcoat of police blue. That coat was remarkable in itself, a coat which no other man in London, save a member of her Majesty's constabulary would have been entitled to wear without attracting the charge of impersonating a police officer, for it was indeed standard police issue, made from standard police blue serge. The coat was a gift from Chief Inspector Legrange of the Yard, presented to Soames with gratitude and much ceremony following his timely and inspired intervention during the investigation of the Whitechapel murders.

The fact that Soames was wearing the coat at all on that night was itself worthy of mention, as he was singularly ill-disposed to the garment, and seldom wore it in public because, as he said himself, it made him "look like a cleric, and a sinister cleric at that." On that particular night, the coat had been liberated from its mothballs, I recall, because his favourite outer garment, the ulster, had been dispatched to the seamstress for some running repairs, long overdue.

We had been attending a rare social occasion hosted by Scotland Yard, a social occasion which the populace delight in calling "a policeman's ball" but which would be best described as "a policeman's brawl" there being so much malicious gossip exchanged. Strong drink, as we all know, loosens the most taciturn of tongues, giving rise to much jealous resentment which in turn can result in gratuitous vilification of superiors and the most outrageous slanders and character assassination of work-a-day colleagues. Indeed, even Legrange himself, now a highly respected chief inspector with an unimpeachable reputation, was the subject of certain scurrilous rumours that night.

Soames, as I have said, was examining the body on the floor. It was the body of a man in his late thirties or early forties. He lay on his side, close to the window, his eyes open, an almost comical look of shocked surprise on his face. He had sustained a blow to the head, and there was blood on his face, in his hair and his moustache. Clutched in his right hand was a short walking-stick with a metal tip and a handle of ivory. He was dressed in a tweed suit that had seen better days.

I estimated that the unfortunate man had been dead but a short while – perhaps less than two hours. I could tell that simply from the degree of maculation of the skin, although I would certainly have been able to refine my estimate if Soames had permitted a measurement of body temperature when first we entered the room.

That the murdered man came to the attention of Herbert Soames at all was entirely fortuitous and was due to the fact that Soames and I had decided to walk home that night, which decision was in turn largely due to the unseasonable clemency of the weather, together with the fact that the aforementioned social occasion took place in the Imperial Hotel Pelham Court, which is but a short distance from Barber Street, where Soames and I had rooms.

Passing by the scene of the crime, and seeing that the front door was wide open and the lamps lit, Soames immediately suspected that something was amiss within. I was inclined to pass on by, but Soames bounded up the steps without a second thought. We entered the building and found an open apartment on the ground floor, the dead man on the carpet in the front parlour.

Although there was a bright moon shining outside, the room was dark, the single large window being obscured by heavy curtains. I drew the curtains to throw more light on the scene, whereupon Soames immediately signalled his disapproval with that clicking of his tongue which I find so irritating.

"I thought you would appreciate some more light," I said.

"The light is welcome, Wilson, but not the dust. Observe how much dust you have disturbed."

Right enough, the rays of the moon, which were now streaming in through the window, illuminated a hundred thousand dancing dust particles.

"Sorry, Soames," I said, suitably chastened.

Soames shook his head dismissively. He had forgotten the incident already. His great mind was working on the puzzle before him.

"This man is from out of town," he said.

I was not over-surprised by this revelation. The man was dressed for the street in a heavy tweed suit. "You don't say," I responded.

He nodded. "The cut of his tweed is certainly not the work of a London tailor. I would hazard Devon or Cornwall."

"Not Somerset?" I suggested. This was an attempt at humour. Pretty feeble, I admit, but the hour was late.

"Yes, possibly," Soames conceded. "The south coast, certainly."

The man's hat had fallen off as he fell, and lay, battered and torn, some three feet removed. I examined it.

"Kent," I said.

"I think we have established that he comes from the south coast," said Soames rather testily.

"There is a return railway ticket to Dover in his hatband," I said. I removed the ticket and handed it to Soames.

Soames nodded briskly. "Well spotted, Wilson. You will observe that the ticket is for a day journey from Dover to London and back."

"So the journey started in Dover."

"Indeed. Also, the ticket bears only one ticket collector's punch mark."

"Which means that he had completed only the outward half of the journey."

"Precisely so, Wilson. Now tell me, what do you make of his shoes?"

"I really cannot say, Soames," I replied. "They are quite obscured by mud." The man's shoes were caked in dried grey mud, making it impossible to discern any detail.

"Yes, Wilson, precisely so. And what can you deduce from the mud?"

"He was a man without regard for his personal appearance?"

"On the contrary, my dear Wilson. The condition of his suit and his elaborate moustache tell us otherwise. Take a closer look at the shoes."

I crouched down and examined the man's shoes from close quarters. I could see small pieces of straw mixed in with the mud, and I detected a distinctly unpleasant odour.

"I see pieces of straw," I said.

"And what does that suggest?"

"I am not sure, Soames. Perhaps he walked across rough ground?"

"What about the odour?"

"A musty, earthy smell, like mushroom compost." I shrugged and stood up, my weary knees complaining of my recent unaccustomed posture.

"The smell of rotting vegetation, Wilson. Rotting straw, to be exact. Don't you see? This man spent a lot of his time in the company of animals."

"Animals?"

"Ruminants, Wilson. Herbivores."

"Cattle. A farmer, then?" I mused.

"An animal trainer, I think, Wilson." There was a glint of self-satisfaction in Soames's eye.

"Horses?"

"Something more exotic, Wilson. Take a look at the cane."

"I see nothing remarkable, Soames. A walking-stick like any other. The ivory handle is quite attractive."

"That is no walking-stick, Wilson. It is far too short. And take a look at the metal point on the tip, and the small hook. Now tell me what you see."

Quite suddenly, all the memories of my childhood in South Africa came flooding back to me. I recognized the traditional *ankus*, used by the natives to control their animals. Elephants are notoriously difficult to deal with, having particularly small brains and a characteristically stubborn disposition. The point of the *ankus* encourages them forwards, the hook, which is designed to fit into a small fold of skin just behind the ear, is used for directional control. I smiled broadly at the memory, and Soames laughed aloud. He often feigns impatience at my oafishness, but secretly, I think he enjoys watching the light of realization slowly dawn in the gloom of my ignorance.

"Elephants!" I cried.

"Of course, Wilson. Pachyderms. Now, what of the murder weapon? Take a look around and see what you can find."

"What are we looking for, Soames?" I asked.

"I don't know yet, Wilson. A bludgeon or a blunt instrument of some kind, I expect. Possibly a heavy ornament or a small piece of furniture."

I began a systematic search of the room. There was nothing to be seen which could have been used as a bludgeon. In fact, there was very little of furniture and no ornament of any kind in the room. There was a bookcase behind the door filled with cheap fiction, Dickens and the like, and a heavy-set tall-boy of dubious origin covered in ornate carvings. The drawers of the tall-boy were all empty. The mantle over the fireplace was bare.

I soon grew weary of the search, since there were so few possible hiding places to investigate. Soames, however, continued to exercise his magnifier in a minute examination of every square inch of the room, paying particular close attention to the exposed floorboards which bordered the carpet and the wooden panelling along the inner wall.

It was at this time that I noticed the black hilt of a dagger protruding from the dead man's back, right between the shoulder blades. It was about four inches long, suggesting a blade of perhaps six inches. I pointed it out to Soames.

"Well spotted, Wilson," said Soames without looking up.

"Perhaps you could explain to me why we are looking for a bludgeon, old friend," I said, "when there is a large blade buried close to the man's scapula." I really thought I had caught him out at last.

"Observe the pattern of the blood, my friend," Soames continued without interrupting his work. "See how it emanates from the region of the head, and notice how little blood has come from the stab wound."

Soames's observations were accurate as usual – and obvious, now that he had pointed them out. I said: "So the blows to the cranium killed him? The dagger blow was struck after death?"

"Precisely so, Wilson. It is clear that his heart had stopped by the time he was stabbed. Furthermore, you will notice that the blow that caused the most damage is the one on the crown of his head. This was undoubtedly the blow that killed him, delivered from above and with murderous force."

"So why was the dagger employed at all?"

"That is one of the mysteries which remains to be solved," said Soames with obvious pleasure. "Now come and take a look at this powder residue."

Soames pointed out some small traces of a fine brown-white powder engrained between the fibres of the carpet. I scraped some of the powder onto the blade of my fruit knife and examined it closely.

"An opiate?" I was guessing, for in truth there was so little of the substance present that I doubt if I could have identified it accurately even with the aid of a well-equipped laboratory.

"I think so, Soames. Opium to be exact."

I had no reason to doubt Soames's judgment, since he has more than a passing personal acquaintance with the substance mentioned, together with an enviable reputation in the field of forensic chemistry.

"I think I should check out the rest of the building," I said.

"Good man. Go to it." He patted me on the back. "But keep your revolver handy."

Soames and I both possess revolvers, and Soames is a crack shot, but he seems to have a distaste for firearms, for he only ever carries his when he is anticipating trouble. I, on the other hand, always carry mine with me. It is a habit I picked up in Africa and there have been several occasions in the recent past when Soames and I were each glad of it, even in the civilized surroundings of modern day London.

It was a big house, built in the previous century and on the grand scale. It was deserted, and judging by the general lack of furniture, and the state of the décor, had not been lived in for some time. I returned to the first floor parlour and told Soames what I had discovered.

Soames fell into a deep silence while he pondered the information I had given him. He paced the floor. Back and forth he paced, his brow furrowed, his hands moving in silent discourse with himself. From time to time, he stopped and raised a finger as if he were about to make a pronouncement, only to shake his head and return once more to his ambulatory ruminations.

Eventually, Soames said: "A dwarf!" in much the same way that Pythagoras in his bath must have said "Eureka!" when he was visited by that celebrated flash of inspiration which led him to invent the lightning conductor.

"I beg your pardon, Soames?"

"Come over here, Wilson. Stand close and I will demonstrate."

Soames is certainly a remarkable detective. There are few others like him, and I have nothing but admiration for his deductive powers, but he has a flair for the dramatic and a fondness for endless explanation which I sometimes find wearisome. There are times when I wish he would just tell me what he knows without explaining every minute twist and turn of the deductive reasoning trail, although I admit that others seem to find that whole process fascinating.

"First, take a look at this impression in the dust of the floorboards. Do you see it?"

The impression was very small, barely visible and could have been a mere trick of the light. "A footprint?" I surmised.

"Certainly," said Soames. "And see how small it is. Now come over here and take a look at this mark in the wood panelling."

I looked. "Made by a knife with a broad blade," I postulated.

Soames nodded. "And here is another, and another on the back of the door."

"So there was a knife fight?"

"Yes. But not of the usual hand to hand kind. If you look closely at the marks you will see that they were all made by identical weapons. Also, by the depth of the scars and the orientation of the blades at entry, it is evident that on each occasion the knives were thrown, not thrust into the wall or the door."

"Thrown?"

"Yes. And there is something else, Wilson. If you examine the marks closely, you will observe that on each occasion the blade was inclined at an upward angle at entry."

"I am not sure I follow you, Soames ..."

"The angle of entry is about twenty degrees below horizontal, which proves that each knife was rising when it hit the wall and the door. Assuming that whoever threw them was standing in the centre of the room, roughly where you are now, and that they were thrown from about shoulder height ..."

"They must have been thrown by a ..."

"By a dwarf. Yes."

"Are you suggesting that our friend the elephant trainer was killed by a dwarf who first tried throwing knives at him, and then bludgeoned him to death, and finally stabbed him in the back just to be sure?"

"Obviously the murder was committed by a very tall man, Wilson – remember the initial downward blow to the crown of his head – but there was a dwarf with a knife involved somehow. I am certain of that."

"Or a child?" I said, helpfully.

"I think not," Soames replied.

"So the room was filled with circus performers. I suppose the bearded lady distracted his attention while the strong man hit him over the head with his barbells."

"That is not as outlandish as it sounds," said Soames.

***

Soames asked me to go out and find a newspaper from Kent, and I was glad to undertake the errand, being in need of some fresh air. In spite of the lateness of the hour, I had no difficulty finding a number of newsmongers still open for business, but it took some time to locate one that stocked a newspaper from Kent. It was well over an hour by the time I made it back to the building. As I rounded the corner into the street, I recognized Legrange's carriage outside the house, and there was a small crowd of curiosity seekers assembled on the pavement near the front door.

Two police constables were emerging from the building with a stretcher on which they carried the dead body covered in a large police overcoat of blue serge.

Upstairs, Legrange and Soames stood facing one another across the bloodstain on the carpet. Legrange was whistling through the gap in his front teeth in that irritating tuneless way that he often does when marking time. Soames was silent and tight-lipped. He was no longer wearing his blue serge greatcoat.

I entered with the newspaper. "It's last week's paper, Soames. Sorry about that, but they had nothing more recent."

"Last week is perfect, Wilson." Soames grabbed it from me impatiently. "But what on Earth kept you? Chief Inspector Legrange is waiting for the name."

"The name?" I echoed, nonplussed.

"The name of the victim," Soames replied.

"And the name of the perpetrator, I trust," Legrange added.

Soames leafed quickly through the newspaper. Then he said: "Ah! Here it is. Legrange, fetch out your notebook, moisten your pencil. Here are the names. The victim was Alexander Hibbert, elephant trainer. The murderers, the Castrati Brothers, Milo and Melo."

"Alexander 'ibbert the helephant trainer." Legrange began writing in his notebook. "Be so good as to spell 'ibbert." Soames obliged. "And the Castrati Brothers, was it?"

"Milo and Melo," said Soames. He handed me the newspaper, and fumbled in his waistcoat for his pipe. I could restrain my curiosity no longer. I looked at the page which Soames had found so informative, and there it was – an advertisement for Hopkins Circus, recently returned from a tour of the Continent, starring the flying Castillos, trapeze artists, Alexander Hibbert and his elephant troupe, Count Vostok the Russian clown and of course, Milo and Melo, the Castrati Twins, midget acrobats and knife throwers.

"Right," said Legrange. "Thank you very much Mr. Soames. I can take it from 'ere. I'll keep the newspaper if you don't mind, Doctor Wilson."

***

After Legrange had gone, Soames and I walked the short distance back to Barber Street. All around us, the great city was stirring. A foggy dawn was approaching, and the wet cobblestones at our feet glistened in the fading moonlight. The air was dank and cold.

"We should walk briskly to keep warm," Soames said.

"Perhaps you shouldn't have surrendered your greatcoat on such a night," I replied.

"I will not miss it," said Soames.

We set out at a brisk pace, and Soames filled in the missing pieces of the puzzle for me.

"The house itself was a major clue," he said. "I reasoned that it must be owned by a very wealthy man. Who but a wealthy man can keep a large house in a fashionable quarter of London these days? And who but a very wealthy man can keep such a house empty for extended periods?"

"So who is this wealthy man, Soames?"

"Who knows?" Soames replied. "Undoubtedly some leader of the criminal underclass. I expect Legrange will run him to ground."

"An opium dealer, perhaps," I suggested.

"Exactly my thought, Wilson."

"And what was the elephant trainer doing in the house?"

"We must assume he was on some criminal errand. Delivering a consignment of opium, perhaps – opium smuggled in from the Continent through the port of Dover."

"You told Legrange that the murder was committed by the Castrati midgets."

"Yes, as it was."

"So there was more than one dwarf in the room?"

"Two of them."

"But I thought we decided that the elephant trainer must have been killed by a taller man? Are you saying now that one of the dwarves was responsible?"

"Not one, my dear Wilson. Both of them."

"I do not follow you, Soames."

"Hibbert was a tall man, so we can take it that neither of the dwarves would have been tall enough alone, to strike him with lethal force on the crown of his head."

"So they must have used their combined height ..."

"Precisely, Wilson. They are acrobats, after all. What could be simpler than for one dwarf to jump onto the shoulders of the other to strike the fatal blow?"

"And what of motive, Soames?"

"Greed, Wilson, greed. The basest of all human motives. I would guess that Hibbert came to the house to hand over a consignment of opium and that the dwarves followed him to London and into this room, where they killed him for the money which he received in payment."

"So why would the Castrati Brothers stick a knife in the back of their victim, when he was already dead and the knife would surely implicate them?"

"The dagger was not one of theirs," Soames explained. "It has a narrow blade and is of a type with which I am familiar. I recognized it from the hilt as soon as I saw it. It is a Russian Vladnistikov."

"The clown was Russian, if I remember correctly," I said.

"Yes, Count Vostok. I am slightly acquainted with his family. A man of noble birth, distantly related to the Tsar."

"So it was his dagger?"

"Almost certainly."

"And was he present? Is he a suspect?"

- "He may have been present, Wilson, but be assured he had no hand or part in the murder. The dagger was used to throw suspicion onto him."

"But how can you be sure that he is innocent, Soames?"

"It is unthinkable that a man of high noble blood like the Count could stoop to such a sordid crime as murder, much less the murder of a common criminal."

"Legrange may take a different view when he finds the dagger buried in Hibbert's back," I said.

"He will not find it," Soames replied.

"Why not?"

"Because," said Soames, "I have it here." And he showed me the dagger which was concealed in the sleeve of his jacket.

I must admit that I was shocked by this revelation, and more than a little surprised by my companion's blind faith in the virtues of the Russian aristocracy, but I gave no indication of my misgivings to Soames. After a moment's thought I said: "Perhaps the dwarves were the smugglers and Hibbert followed them to London intending to steal the money, and the dwarves turned the tables on him and killed him."

"Perhaps," Soames conceded. "Either way, you may be certain that a large sum of money was involved."

"Where is this money now, Soames?"

"Clearly one of the players has absconded with it."

"The murderers?"

"Possibly, or maybe the opium dealer."

"We shall have to wait for the trial to find out," I said.

Soames shook his head. "The case will never come to trial, Wilson."

Again, I was shocked. "Whyever not, Soames?"

Soames smiled. "Evidently, one of the dwarves struck the fatal blow, and is guilty of murder. Yes?"

"Yes."

"And the other dwarf, the one who provided the platform for his brother, what is he guilty of?"

I pondered this question before answering: "Accessory to murder, I suppose."

"At worst, Wilson. I'll wager a good lawyer could argue that he played no part in the action of his brother."

"Yes, I can see that, Soames, but the one who struck the blow is guilty of a heinous murder and must hang for it."

Soames nodded. "Evidently, but how will Legrange find out which one that was? We may assume that the murder weapon is at the bottom of the Thames and will never be found, and there were no witnesses that we know of."

"I see. There is no way that Legrange will ever be able to separate the guilty from the innocent, so he will have to let them both go free?"

"Indubitably, my dear Wilson," said Soames.

I hate it when he says that.

MILLINGTON'S LAST GAME

First Published in the 2012 SciFi Anthology

How about a game of chess?
I don't think so.
What's the score so far?
We've played 300 games, give or take.
How many have I won?
None.
Losses?
None.
All draws, huh?
Pretty much.
What about Commander Millington?
Millington beat me in 3,587 games.
Out of how many?
3,613.
Draws?
Twenty-four.
That leaves you with how many wins?
Do the math yourself.
Two?
Two.
You're not counting the last game, are you?

Why shouldn't I? He resigned.

He *died*. That's hardly the same thing.

The game was adjourned. I won by default. He went for a spacewalk and never came back. Those are the rules.

***

Open a channel, Sam.

Channel Open. Record On.

This is Gemini Deep Space Mission, day 1473. Transmitting from 30778 parsecs. Acting Commander George Dutton. All systems nominal. Acceleration constant at 1.0072 gravities. Velocity 0.0669 light. Estimated time to destination: 707 Gemini days. Nothing exceptional to report. Weather sunny, no cloud cover. Over.

Why do you always say that?

A little humor does no harm.

Crackle... crackle... sssssssssssssssssssssssssss.

I hear nothing, George.

Quiet!

There's nothing to hear, George.

sssssssssssssssssssssssssssssss.

sssssssssssssssssssssssssssssss.

Close the channel, Sam.

Record Off. Channel Closed.

I'm scared, Sam.

Why?

What if ... what if they're all gone?

Mission control, you mean?

Everyone.

What, some global disaster?

Yeah, a nuclear war, an asteroid hit or something.

The roaches will have taken over. Giant roaches everywhere, running everything. King Roach in the White House.

That's not funny, Sam.

Please yourself.

Who decided to give you a sense of humor, anyhow?

***

How about a game of chess, Sam? I'll be white. Pawn to king four.

Pawn to king four.

Looks like a draw.

Why do you always do that? We could play the game out.

It was bad enough losing to the commander. How d'you think I'd feel if I lost to a machine?

***

Talk to me, George.

What d'you want me to say?

Tell me about Debbie.

I've told you everything about her a thousand times.

Tell me again.

Why?

It's good for your mental health.

She's three years old.

Was.

Don't interrupt. She has blonde curls—

Had.

Shut up!

How old would she be now?

In *our* now, she's seven.

And in reality? How old is she in reality?

What does that mean?

If she sent us a message today, how old would she say she was?

Maybe eight, but she'd be nearly nine by the time we got the message.

That's a guess, right?

No. I've done the math. Check it if you like.

What about her mother?

Sylvia must be thirty-seven. A year older than me, now.

***

Play it again, Sam. Play the recording.

We've listened to it a hundred times already.

Just once more, please, Sam.

He's gone, George. He's not coming back.

Computer, reload mission record index 373.

Commander Millington can you hear me?

Yes George, loud and clear. I'm just about to open the outer airlock. All systems are nominal.

Good luck, Commander.

Thanks, George. You're in charge until I get back.

What's it like out there, Commander?

Clear black sky. Lots of stars. No moon.

Any sign of rain?

Sorry, George, I didn't catch that.

Not important, sir. Where are you?

I'm close to the antenna.

How does it look?

It's out of alignment, but it looks undamaged

...

It's fixed. I'm on my way back.

Take your time, Commander.

I'll give you the word when to open the airlock.

...

George, my air supply is failing fast (cough). Switching to back-up supply.

Roger that, Commander.

...

Commander?

(cough) My back-up supply is—

Commander Millington? Come in, Commander!

(wheeze) George, what have you done?

What really happened to the commander, George?

He was unlucky, Sam. A chance event. Nothing I could've done about it.

All the evidence points to murder.

That's crap.

Is it?

Sure. It was an accident. In space, accidents happen all the time.

His suit failed.

Yes. One of the suits was faulty. He chose the wrong one, that's all.

So how come that suit was faulty? I think someone interfered with it.

You mean, you think I interfered with it.

Did you?

What if I did?

You killed him. You murdered the commander.

No, I'm not a killer.

Okay, so explain what you did.

Go to hell.

Tell it like you would to a board of enquiry. George Dutton, Acting Commander of the Gemini Deep Space Mission, please take the stand—

Go to hell!

—and explain to the members of the board what happened to your mission commander, Rijkart Millington. You were beyond mission commit, nearly four years out—close to one light year—when there was an accident.

We lost antenna alignment.

Your antenna was struck by a piece of space debris at high velocity.

Yes, Admiral. We adjourned our game.

Game?

We were playing chess.

I see. Continue.

Commander Millington went out to fix the antenna.

And his suit malfunctioned.

Yes, sir. He had successfully realigned the antenna and started back when—

His air supply ran out.

Yes sir.

How long was he out?

Not long. Maybe twenty minutes.

If memory serves me, these suits hold enough oxygen for a couple of hours.

Yes, sir.

And yet it ran out after twenty minutes.

Roughly, sir, yes.

These suits have an emergency back-up supply. Am I right, Acting Commander?

Yes, sir.

And that failed too?

Correct, sir.

And you lost Commander Millington.

He drifted away from the ship. Slowly. I saw him. I watched him drift away. Spinning. It was several hours before I lost sight of him.

You had a second suit.

Yes, sir.

Fully functional.

Yes, sir.

So, you could have gone out after him.

I could have. Yes, sir, but—

But you didn't.

It was my judgment that a rescue attempt would have placed the entire mission in jeopardy. How could I leave the ship unmanned?

Can you offer any explanation for how Commander Millington's spacesuit failed so catastrophically?

It was a chance event, sir.

Explain that.

Just drop it, Sam. I don't want to talk about it anymore.

***

You know you're going to turn the ship around.

No way.

You have to abort the mission.

I can't abort.

Why not? You heard the order.

It was garbled.

It told you to abort the mission You know that's what it said.

Maybe, but the signal was scrambled. It could've been anything.

Like what?

I don't know. Anything.

You're crazy. Mission Control has ordered you to turn around and go home. What's the matter with you? Don't you want to go home?

I'm the mission commander—

Acting.

—and I will carry on to the final destination.

Don't I have a vote?

No, you're a computer.

You're crazy!

I will complete the mission.

For heaven's sake! Why?

What do you think I'll find if I go back?

A hero's welcome. A tickertape parade up Fifth Avenue.

What about my friends and relatives?

They'll be there, waiting.

Most of them will be dead.

Maybe. You can't know that for sure, George.

Debbie...

She'll be grown up. Maybe have children of her own.

Her mother will be dead. Dead and buried.

Everyone dies, George.

If Debbie ever sees me again, she's gonna hate me.

Why?

Because.

Because what?

Just because.

You're being childish.

Because I went away and abandoned her, that's why.

Is that what's bugging you?

Yes, but there's something else.

What is it?

She'll be ...

What? She'll be what, George? Finish your sentences.

She'll be old.

So what? You'll be old too.

Yes, but she'll be older than me.

That's crazy. It's not possible.

I've done the math. If I turn back today, I'll be in my early fifties by the time I get back. Debbie'll be in her sixties. She'll be older than me, older than her own father!

***

It was a chance event, you say.

Explain.

Only one of the suits was faulty. Commander Millington could have chosen the other one. The two suits were interchangeable. They looked identical. He had a choice.

And that's what you mean by a chance event?

Sure. Also, he could have ordered me to realign the antenna. So he had a three in four chance of living. He was unlucky. He made the wrong choice—twice. Chance killed him.

What would have happened if Millington had sent you out?

I would have died.

Millington would have aborted the mission.

Maybe.

No way he would have continued on his own.

Maybe. We'll never know.

What if you had selected the good suit?

I wouldn't have.

Why not?

I knew which one was faulty.

All right, what if Millington had chosen the good suit?

He would have survived.

Would he?

Probably.

***

What are you doing, George?

Remembering.

Debbie on that long sandy beach?

Yes. The sun's warm, the ocean gently lapping. Her mother's lying by my side on the sand, most of her body under an umbrella.

Her legs are getting burnt, George. I see a mountain in the distance.

Debbie's in a field, jumping on a haystack. She's laughing. I'm thinking she needs to settle down. She'll burst a blood vessel or something, she's laughing so hard. Sylvia's watching. She's smiling.

She doesn't see the danger. Now Debbie's paddling in the water; wearing a pink hat.

If I use my hands to blank out the scene on both sides, there's just Debbie and the vast ocean.

I see her, George. I see her! Nothing overhead but the blue sky and deep space beyond. Each time she comes down, she topples over into the hay. Her face is red. She's laughing fit to burst.

I bet she'll remember that day until she dies.

Don't you want to go home, George?

More than anything, Sam. I'd give anything to go back, but that's impossible. Don't you see? This is a one-way trip. Always was.

I wish you'd turn the ship around, George.

Why? Why do you care either way?

She's my daughter too, George.

ABOUT JJ TONER

JJ Toner writes short stories and novels. Most of his published books are WW2 spy stories, but his first love has always been Science Fiction. He is working on a new series called Android Wars. JJ lives in Ireland.

Website: JJToner.com

BOOKS BY JJ TONER

Houdini's Handcuffs, a Noir Detective Thriller, featuring DI Ben Jordan
Find Emily, a second DI Jordan Detective Thriller
Retribution and Other Stories, Short Stories

The Black Orchestra, a WW2 spy thriller
The Wings of the Eagle, the second WW2 Spy Thriller in the Black Orchestra series
A Postcard from Hamburg, the third WW2 Spy Thriller in the series
The Gingerbread Spy, the fourth WW2 Spy Thriller in the series
The Serpent's Egg, Red Orchestra WW2 Spy Thriller
Liberation Berlin, a WW2 novel

Zugzwang, a pre-war detective story featuring Kommissar Saxon
Queen Sacrifice, a second case for Kommissar Saxon
The White Knight, a third case for Kommissar Saxon

EGGS and Other Stories, a collection of fun SF short stories

The Shape of Fear – Android Wars book 1
Escape from Luciflex – Android Wars book 2